To all the courageous men and women who have allowed me to walk alongside them on their journey through dementia.

Pam & David

Remember Remember

HAZEL McHAFFIE

warm wishes,

Hazel

Luath Press Limited

EDINBURGH

www.luath.co.uk

First published 2010

ISBN: 978-1-906817-29-9

The author's right to be identified as author of this book under the
Copyright, Designs and Patents Act 1988 has been asserted.

The publisher acknowledges the support of

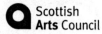 Scottish
Arts Council

towards the publication of this volume.

The paper used in this book is recyclable.
It is made from low chlorine pulps
produced in a low energy, low emissions manner
from renewable forests.

Printed and bound by Bell & Bain Ltd., Glasgow

Typeset in 10.5 point Sabon

Acknowledgements

Without the generosity of many people living with dementia I would never have been able to write this book. They have taught me more than they ever knew and it has been a privilege to be part of their lives. Respect for their rights to privacy precludes me from naming them but I thank them all comprehensively. Random conversations with numerous people involved in the care of people with dementia, in homes and organisations, over decades have also helped to shape my thinking. I am constantly amazed by them.

Dr Gwen Turner and Dr Richard Turner, who have a wealth of personal as well as clinical experience between them, gave me invaluable advice on an early manuscript which helped to shape the final version of this story, and I thank them warmly for their friendship and expert help. Professor Tony Hope is one of the most encouraging people I know, and I'm indebted to him for his ongoing support and reassurance, particularly at a time when he was working on his own major report about the ethical issues associated with dementia.

I'm grateful too to the team at Luath Press, and in particular, to my editor, Jennie Renton, who highlighted my faults but left me to correct them – exactly the right way to handle me! Nele Andersch proved a real friend when I needed one.

And as always, I am indebted to my family for their constant support and love. Jonathan, Rosalyn and Camille read drafts with affectionate prejudice. David meticulously proof-read the final version and gave me the space I needed to get lost in this story.

Family tree found in a handbag at Bradley Drive

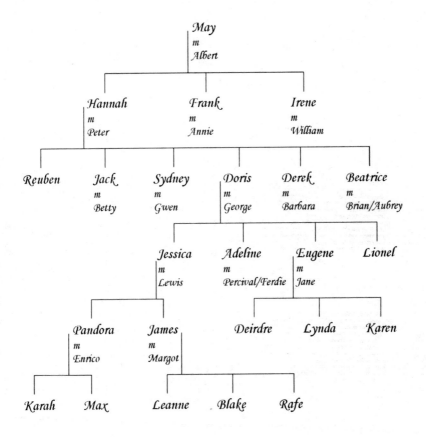

Prologue

SIMON ARRIVED EARLY for his lecture. He wanted time to size up his student audience and plan his tactics.

As the latecomers slouched in, his brain rehearsed details of the case he intended to present. He'd need to tread extra warily – too much information could so easily betray confidences.

Professor Duncan was on his feet; the buzz of young voices died.

'Good morning. May I remind you to switch off your mobile phones, please. I'm sure the world can cope without your pearls of wisdom for 90 minutes on this particular Thursday morning.' A pause while everyone checked. 'Thank you. I can assure you the sense of bereavement will soon be forgotten, because our guest speaker today is Simon Montgomery-Bates. As a practising lawyer, author of six legal texts, and with something of a reputation as an after-dinner speaker, he brings a wealth of experience and skill to his presentations. I can promise you, you will be challenged, you may be shocked, but you will not be dozing during *this* session. And that includes you three on the back row who seem to be settling down for some kind of slumber party.' A ripple of appreciation. 'So, without further ado, Simon.'

Simon strolled forward, adjusting his bow tie, and let his gaze wander over the faces. Only when he had their full attention did he start to speak. He began to pace, one hand behind his back, the other clutching his lapel. All eyes followed him.

'Ladies and gentlemen, the case I bring before you today bears all the hallmarks of a *cause célèbre*. We have an elderly widow with aristocratic connections and inherited wealth. We have attempted murder.' A pause. 'We have a lawyer-lover with a conflict of interests... no, not me, I can assure you! We have issues of mental competence; a cuckoo in the nest; tension between potential inheritors; a will that must remain sealed until the testator dies; secrets and deceptions that span decades. And yet,' he raised one finger, 'this is an ordinary family. They might be living next door to you... or to me. (Contrary to campus rumour, I do inhabit this planet, despite my Vulcan-like logic and detachment.) It's highly unlikely that the names of any of these people will hit the headlines, or that they will ever appear before you in the High Court. Nevertheless, their situation poses a number of legal challenges.

'We'll begin with the eldest daughter of the widow, Annie. And before you start texting the *News of the World*, Annie is, of course, not her real name. Annie is in her sixties and in the process of clearing the family home. You... yes, the young lady there, in the red jumper... you are Annie. You grew up in this house. You love every stone of it. It's full of memories. How are you feeling, dismantling your history?'

'Sad? Angry? Torn?'

'Indeed. I'm glad you included angry, because you have a brother and a sister who also grew up in this house, but they...'

JESSICA

Chapter 1

IT WAS IN THIS room that I almost murdered my mother.

My hands were actually starting to press down on her shoulders. As she sank she grabbed for the rail, missed, and began to flounder. A wave of water went over the side of the bath, soap stung my eye. I groped for the towel. By the time I could see again my rage had passed.

Looking back now, I still wonder. Would it have been better to have ended it that day? Maybe once this house is sold I shall get some kind of resolution.

The bathrooms were top priority as soon as Mother was admitted to the home. It was the smell; no amount of scrubbing or bleach would eradicate it. Floors, suites, tiles, everything had to go.

It's a big concession having men in to do the tiling. But James was insistent. 'OK, do the painting and papering yourself, if you must, but let me organise the bathrooms.'

They're only young, Jake and Richie, fingernails encrusted with grout, but in a few hours they've finished upstairs and down. No cracks, no misalignments.

'Nice choice, Mrs B,' Jake said. 'Can't go wrong with white.'

Oh yes you can. Mother had white in here before…

'We'll be back tomorrow to finish the grouting. You'll be all hunky-dory by teatime.'

But I'll be glad when they've gone. It's painful having strangers in this house that's so full of family ghosts.

It's not the same for James.

I can see her now, the week before she was admitted to The Morningside. Hard to believe it's been almost a year.

It was such a warm day for March I wanted to fling open all the doors and windows… except that anything open represented an escape route to my mother. She shuffled into the hall and stood passively, waiting to be led. I took her hand and inched her from room to room, willing the old familiarity to spark something in her brain.

But a packet of Ginger Nut biscuits lying on the kitchen surface generated more interest than any of my prompts. She spent 10 minutes trying to pick a flower off an embroidered cushion. I tried to distract her, like they said, showed her family photographs: no response.

The last time she'd been in this house she'd given the appearance of knowing where she was. Now even that veneer had gone. Hope died within me.

Now I have the house to myself again, I can get on with emptying cabinets. At least the kitchen doesn't need redecorating having been completely gutted and refitted after the fire.

It had a fair hold before Bert, the postman, called the Fire Brigade. Bert knew all about Mother and when he'd smelt burning he'd charged straight into the house to check she was safe. It was empty. Mother was skulking behind the garden shed, a singed teacloth in her hand. 'Have you come for tea?'

She'd left an empty saucepan on the electric ring, the fire chief said, then she'd dumped a pile of towels and teacloths on top of it.

'She has Alzheimer's,' I explained.

'And she lives on her own?'

The criticism stung. I'd already removed bleach, medicines, matches, scissors and knives. I visited her daily, cooked, cleaned, ironed, shopped, stuck labels on everything to remind her what it was. I phoned her frequently to check she was still there, still pretending.

It was a bleak moment standing there amidst the devastation she'd caused, facing the only possible solution.

On paper, of course, I was not alone with this.

When the diagnosis was finally pronounced my uncles, Sydney and Derek, did visit, together for moral support. But Mother dredged up an Oscar-winning performance. Her only sister, Beatrice, who saw more of the deterioration, spent so much time talking about *her* ailments and *her* activities it was doubtful whether she even registered the implications of the illness.

To an extent I could excuse that generation on account of their own advancing years, but I've felt far less forgiving of my own. Eugene, living in Australia, had a cast-iron reason for leaving things to me. And to be fair, he rang, he commiserated, he suggested buying in help, offered financial assistance. My younger sister, Adeline, technically should have shared the responsibility. Technically. She has more money (she works in advertising; her salary is obscene) and more time (no children or grandchildren). But in her position, she 'cannot afford' the slightest whiff of anything 'unsavoury' in her background.

And so I'm the one still taking responsibility for Mother. She may no longer be physically in my charge, but her house is.

The task of getting it into order was overwhelming, so I'm tackling a room at a time. Kitchen first – least demanding, least emotionally draining. Anything I find in these cupboards got there within the space of eleven months – the time I lived here with Mother after the fire. I make rapid progress. Cooking paraphernalia... charity shop. Shrivelled vegetables, dubious packets and tubs, glue dots, erasers, half-eaten biscuits, sticky jelly babies... straight in the bin. Nothing of any significance. Then, at the back of one of the base units, I find a box tied up with string, the knot so intricate that Houdini would have been daunted. I resort to scissors. It feels sacrilegious.

Inside I find... a treasure trove. Drawings by grandchildren; an invitation to an art exhibition in Glasgow; a school note saying Eugene has won a special Governors' 'Overall Improvement' prize; a newspaper clipping showing Adeline and me holding a turnip at some agricultural show; a bundle of letters held together with a red elastic band (assorted senders: Grandmamma, Lionel, the Palace of Holyrood, me, the electricity company, social services, James, Jenners, George)...

I close the shoebox and carry it through to the hall. So many stories lie in that single hoard. Those impenetrable knots – perhaps this was Mother's way of protecting her past; if she couldn't get into the contents she couldn't destroy them.

Tucked down the side of the adjoining cabinet I find an old sepia photograph of Mother's family. The names are written on the back in a beautiful rolling hand, not hers: *Jack, Sydney, Doris, Derek, Beatrice, Mamma*. But both the name, *Doris*, and her face are covered in heavy ink scratchings. How sad. Was Mother aware that her identity was being eradicated by this crippling illness when she removed herself from the portrait? What must it do to a person to contemplate their own living extinction?

I let my thumb glance over the blackened spot where she once smiled. Doris: eldest daughter, mother, grandmother. It's too easy to forget those years in the ongoing struggle with dementia.

I slip the photo into the shoebox in the hall, my mind still in the past.

The holes in the frame of the front door jerk my mind on to another crisis.

I'd only gone down to the newsagents. Ten minutes running there and back, not stopping to talk to Eunice McClarity, not waiting for the pedestrian lights to turn green. I'd left Mother asleep, knowing I must be back before she wakened.

The futility of trying to fit my key into the keyhole took a while to penetrate. It must fit. It *must!*

I tried a nail file. I tried phoning. I tried an appeal. 'Mother. It's only me, Jessica. Open the door for me, there's a dear.'

I listened through the letterbox. What did silence denote? Unlit gas... electrical sockets... steep stairs... every hazard raced through my mind.

The policeman was sympathetic but brutally pragmatic. 'Only one way in. Break the lock. We cannae just slip a slice of plastic in, and bingo. Doesnae work like that. But I can give you the name of a reliable bloke who'll repair the door.'

I had no choice.

All my anxiety about the trauma of an SAS-style invasion proved groundless. Mother was oblivious to the whole operation, lying fully clothed in two inches of hot water in the bath, her head encased in a towel and fur earmuffs, her slippers soaking in the lavatory pan.

'Did I invite you?' she said – not to the assorted strangers storming her house; to me. Then, 'Ring the pope. He'll know.'

It was the last time I left her unattended.

As I pick up the sack of foodstuffs and drag it to the back door, I can't resist a wry smile at how cross Mother had been that time Pandora tore through her cupboards, 'saving' her from food poisoning.

'In my day there was no such thing as sell-by dates.'

'Gran! It's gross.'

Pandora. Light years away from Mother's chaos. Judged against Pandora's standards we are all incompetent. I wish I could rid myself of this nagging anxiety about my daughter.

But there's work to be done before James arrives to remove the boxes and bags. Dear James. What would I do without him? I know he'll be there until this job is done, whatever his own private reservations.

'Yoo-hoo. Anybody at home?'

'In the kitchen, James,' I sing out.

'Wow, Mum. You've certainly made inroads today.'

'Scrubs up pretty well, huh?'

'Certainly does.'

'I'm impressed. I'll heft these boxes out to the car, then we'll have the space to see what's what.'

He picks up the shoebox.

'Not that one, James.'

'I hope you're not taking more of Gran's junk back to your house,' he says, looking at me sharply.

It's fair enough. I can only pray I live long enough to sort everything out in my own home, so that he's spared this task. I often think Mother will outlast me. She's a tough cookie. She's survived having twice as many children as I had. Her diet has been frugal but wholesome, whereas I've fallen into the bad habit of comfort eating. And her life now is far less stressful than mine. In a way I envy her this final freedom from responsibilities for bills, relationships, tax returns, meals, inherited genes...

But then, she's already paid her dues. As I tried explaining to Aunt Beatrice.

'Remember all the years she struggled. Look at everything she did for everybody else. I want her to have some luxury now.'

'Luxury's wasted on her. So's sacrifice, come to that.'

'Even if *she* doesn't appreciate it, *I* want to know she's getting what she deserves.'

'Doris would have wanted her family to have everything, not to waste money on her.'

I don't tell Beatrice the other reason. The guilt I feel.

Chapter 2

GUILT, REGRET, DESPAIR – I experienced them all in this front bedroom. It was so hard to come back. I thought I'd left it for good when I walked out of it as a bride 40 years before. But that mad autumn there was no other viable option. Neighbours, strangers, the emergency services – it wasn't their responsibility to rescue Mother from the predicaments her chaotic mind got her into and no one else in the family could find space in their lives for her. So that left me.

Having a bolt-hole of my own had become a dangerous indulgence.

Today this room feels naked compared with the rest of the house, although the burgundy throw I brought with me from my own home is still on the bed. The piles of unused gifts, the broken implements, unread magazines, 29 bottles of oil and eleven containers of bleach, boxes of corsets, liberty bodices and vests, Lego, blankets, icing sugar, four wirelesses, a slashed pouffé... all this clutter had to go before I could reach the bed. I couldn't afford to dither around recycling things, I simply pushed everything into the garden shed and disposed of it in the refuse collection surreptitiously, so as not to let another living soul glimpse the extent of the pandemonium in my mother's head. Not even James.

I clung to the hope that, once she settled down with me in constant attendance, she would become more biddable, my dislocation would become more bearable. It never did. I sank exhausted into bed, rarely getting more than a couple of hours' sleep before I was summoned by sounds of the prowling insomniac.

I bundle up the quilt and squash it into a black sack.

The furniture is flimsy in here, but my lower spine still protests as I inch it into the centre of the room. It would make excellent timber for a bonfire. I must ask James. His boys used to love making fires with him at the bottom of the garden. I picture them, swathed in the bright scarves and hats I knitted for them, crouching alongside their father, toasting marshmallows.

Perhaps not. The 'children' are scarcely that any more. Leanne is taller than me now. Blake ended up in a police station in December, for shoplifting a box of Roses chocolates – 'for his nana', he said. And where Blake goes, his younger brother, Rafe, aspires to go.

I peel back the carpet. An antique smell leaks into the room. I throw open the window but once I start to strip off the first sheets of wallpaper, I no longer notice it anyway. This is one DIY job I do enjoy. I don't know why – a psychologist probably would. The paper is so old and dry that it lifts off in crispy swathes.

It bears the marks of nail polish and felt-tip pen and latterly, tomato paste.

Mother was supposed to be dozing in the conservatory. I'd been out in the garden hanging yet another row of sheets on the line, but... the wicker seat was empty. This bedroom was like a scene from Armageddon. I wonder, now, was she trying to paint herself back into her own territory?

From the window I can look down on the garden. The memories are kinder. Mother kneeling on the lawn, weeding; Mother raking the autumn leaves; Mother pushing the children on the swing.

'Higher, Granny D, higher!'

I see Pandora's pigtails being flung around in the sheer effort to touch the sky. I hear my mother's laughter floating across the lawn as she sends her granddaughter swooping upwards, the creak of the chains, the child lifting herself right off the seat, my breath catching in fear.

Pandora. Why did I take so long to notice my daughter's obsessive streak? She has always yearned for prestige, always cared about appearances. Aged eleven she changed the names of the family cats from Poppy and Smudge to Lady Petunia and Lord Montmorency. Should I have insisted she seek professional help when the fads evolved into compulsions? It hurts – both the behaviour, and the responsibility for it.

I keep hoping that age will soften some of the excesses but I see no sign of it. Gym-toned and botox-rigid, she finds my 'slovenliness' a sore trial. She'd like me to be an elegant granny for her children but I do not answer the job description. Privately, I'm a disappointment to myself as well. Why *can't* I manage to keep in shape – mentally and physically? But ageing *is* disappointing. Health fails, memory lets you down, everything sags, the children don't need you, friends die, dreams fade. Maybe Mother's been spared something worse than confusion: clarity of vision! Why don't we revere and respect the elderly in our culture, value their wisdom? Mother is why. I am why.

Pandora has consigned her grandmother to the past tense. I can understand that, but it still hurts. This is her old playmate and ally, the person who used to be first on her prayer list.

Thank goodness for James. He remains totally in league with his beloved Gran. And he seems to know intuitively how to treat her. I've had to learn.

Once we had the diagnosis, they gave me lists: all the things you should never do with someone who has Alzheimer's. Absolutes, they call them.

Never argue; always agree.
Never reason; always divert.

Never lecture; always reassure.
Never condescend; always encourage or praise.
Never force; always reinforce…

Ten commandments. I pinned them up and kept looking at them, catching myself in error at least 15 times a day. They started to sink in… only to desert me when she drove me beyond reason.

Never shame; always distract.

You try not showing disgust when your toes slide into somebody else's poo in your slippers!

Never say 'You can't'; always do what they can do.

When she's brandishing a carving knife? Hello! Reality check!

Never command or demand; always ask.

Yeah, right! 'Mother, would you be a dear and consider letting go of my neck? You seem to be strangling me.'

Never say 'I told you'; always repeat.

Always repeat! How many millions of times can a human being cope with saying, 'No, Mother, you didn't invite me. I'm your daughter, Jessica. This is my home.'

If I hadn't ever heard of the commandments I'd have been spared this additional layer of guilt at least. But it did get easier to trust my instincts and accept compromises. Nothing was going to restore Mother to her pre-dementia lucidity, so I could happily agree to anything. And because she wouldn't either understand or remember what I said, I could release my frustration by adding nonsense of my own.

'*Did I invite you?*'

'No, but do please feel free to invite me in next time you decide to empty all my geraniums into the sink.'

'*Is that you, George?*'

'Well, not last time I looked, but I'll keep checking.'

'*Where's my purse?*'

'Let me see, it might be under the holly bush, or in the bath, or burnt to a cinder. Or it might never have existed.'

As she withdraws further and further from reality, I do

periodically take stock and check that I'm not wandering into unacceptable realms. Especially when she and I are all alone.

Stay calm and patient, they say.

Try that when you're permanently deprived of sleep, tormented and exhausted yourself, *I* say.

Focus on a word or phrase that makes sense, they tell you.

And just how many times a day would that apply to the same word?

There is no off-duty, no annual leave, no retirement. At least there wasn't, until I put Mother into The Morningside.

Which is why I'm stripping this room and closing down the family home.

There, that's the paper all off. A cup of tea calls.

I take the mug outside and look up at the house from the garden seat. It's a solid building, well proportioned. It should fetch a good price. Enough to pay... say it quickly... £968.80 a week – a *week*! £50,000 a year. As long as she doesn't live too long beyond the doctors' predictions, and inflation doesn't double that figure.

Given the sums involved, I needed my siblings to help me make the decision about selling. Eugene left the final word to me.

'Jess, you're the one who's seeing Mother all the time. If it means selling the old house to pay for the care, that's fine by me. You're the boss. I must try to get back before she forgets who I am.'

It's probably too late for that, Eugene. But how about coming for *me*?

My sister, who 'pops up' from London once a year and has never taken responsibility for Mother, didn't let that hold her back.

'I don't know, houses are a sound investment. Once it's sold, that's that. If we hang on to it, it will keep appreciating in value. You could think about letting. There must be a big demand for rented properties in Edinburgh.'

I shouldn't have been surprised. Her response to Mother coming to live with me had been even more breathtaking.

'How about if I try to free up a week in the summer? We could go shopping, do things together like we used to. A bit of retail therapy works wonders.'

'What about Mother?'

'She'd be OK for a couple of hours, wouldn't she?'

'No, Adeline, she would not. She can't be trusted alone for a couple of *minutes,* never mind hours. She needs constant supervision.'

'Oh. I see. Well, why don't we buy in some help for that week? I'll share the cost. They could look after her while I take you out shopping. My treat.'

I kept the explosion for James, who was typically pragmatic.

'Don't give it another thought, Mum. Gran *has* to go into care, and the only way we can afford the kind of care we want for her is to sell her house. Full stop. Adeline's loaded, she doesn't need Gran's money. Uncle Eugene says do what you have to do. You – and Pandora and me – all say, sell up to pay for somewhere decent. End of story.'

Aunt Beatrice rang at 11 in the evening to add her opinion. I'd just battled Mother back into bed for the third time and flew to stop the phone wakening her again.

The preliminaries were cursory. She clearly had an agenda.

'D'you know what's in her will, Jessica?'

'No. Why?'

'What if she's specified who the house goes to?'

'While she's alive her own needs take precedence, surely? Whatever the house makes is for her benefit.'

'You're her executor, aren't you?'

'James and I both are.'

'And that was Doris's choice?'

'It was. We did it all properly when she was perfectly competent to make that decision and hand over power of attorney against the day when she couldn't decide for herself.'

'Hmm.'

'It makes sense, doesn't it? I'm on the spot. And James is good on the money side.'

'And he's your son.'

'But we've consulted Eugene and Adeline on everything. We're presuming Mother will have left the house and her possessions to all three of us children equally – or our heirs. If you know differently, now's the time to say so.'

'It's just that I know Adeline isn't happy.'

My sister was defensive when I reported this conversation.

'I only asked Aunt Beatrice what she thought because you didn't seem to be listening to what I wanted at all.'

'I *was* listening, but all you could talk about was shopping! Mother's a danger to herself and everyone around her these days. I don't seem to be able to get you to accept the fact she needs supervision 24/7. We don't want to dump her in some grotty place.'

'No, of course we don't...'

'Even if we went for no more than the basics, we'd have to sell. I thought you agreed to go for the best. She's our *mother*!'

'Well...'

'She doesn't need her house any more. And it's *her* house. *Her* money. For *her* care.'

'Aunt Beatrice reckons we ought to know what's in the will before we decide.'

'Well, we can't. The lawyer told us that we can't. Mum insisted.'

'You might be going against her wishes.'

'Adeline, if you have a problem with me dealing with Mother's affairs, why don't you come right out with it? I can't be doing with all this...'

'It's not easy, being down here...'

'OK, how about a swap? You come up here and take care of Mother and I'll stay in your flat until you've decided what's best.'

'Don't be silly. What about my job?'

'I used to have a job too, remember? I was a teacher six

years ago.'

'How much money does Mother have in the bank? Is there enough to keep her in the home for a couple of years, and then see if... well, if she's still around?'

'For goodness sake! If James and the lawyers say it isn't enough and we have to sell the house, that's enough for me. This is *James* we're talking about. Her grandson. Look, if you can see any other way of finding the money, then talk to the lawyers yourself. But remember, Mother's still here needing round-the-clock care, so it'd better be this week rather than next year.'

'There's no need to snap, Jessica. I'm only asking. I'm reliant on other people to fill in the gaps.'

'So tell me, what do I do with Mum? Because *something* has to happen. Things can't go on the way they are.'

'Let me think about it. I'll get back to you.'

Adeline has an unnerving ability to shake my confidence. What if Mother *has* left the house to someone specific? I ring the lawyer, but he reiterates: 'Mrs Mannering's stipulation is, none of the family may know the contents of the will while she's alive.' He can't go against that instruction without her consent, and she's in no position to consent to anything, but he confirms that the sale of her house in the current circumstances conforms with the spirit of her wishes.

On hearing that, Adeline sniffed; Aunt Beatrice maintained her silence.

Neither can find a slot in their busy schedules for a trip to Scotland. Not even for shopping.

Today when James arrives, the will crops up in conversation and he has another conundrum for me.

'I'm not sure if I'm meant to tell anybody about this, but since we're talking finance... over the years, sums of money have been deposited in Gran's bank account. Sizeable sums. Anonymously. Do you know anything about them?'

'No.'

'Hmm. Odd.'

'Have you asked the lawyer?'

'Yep, but he doesn't know – or won't say.'

'Maybe it's Adeline's conscience-money!' I say.

'Without broadcasting her generosity? I don't think so.'

'Maybe Mother has a secret admirer.'

'A billionaire toyboy!' he laughs. 'Way to go, Gran!'

'It's not impossible, you know. Just because a woman's past her prime, doesn't mean…' I didn't intend the heat.

I turn away and apply myself to filling another hole.

'Mum?… Do I smell a story?'

'It's nothing.'

'The kind of nothing that makes my mother blush? Come on.'

I can't.

'Unless I'm very much mistaken, this isn't about Gran, is it?'

'It's all in the past now. There's nothing to tell.'

'What's in the past?'

I sigh. 'There was someone. It's over.'

'Someone?'

I turn away, searching for the next crevice. James moves till he's facing me directly.

'So?'

'It's history. The timing was all wrong. Gran needed me.'

'Who was he?'

'A lawyer I met in my solicitor's office. He came from down south, but he was involved in some drawn-out court case up here at the time.'

'Name?'

'Aaron. Aaron Wiseman.'

'So…'

'He was… very kind. And he gave me some good legal advice. And his mother went to the same school as Aunt Beatrice.'

'Small world. I'm surprised she didn't warn him off.'

'James!'

'Sorry.'

'And for the record, his mother said nice things about

Gran. Mum was older but his mother knew her by sight and heard about her after they'd all left school. And it was all complimentary. Or at least the things Aaron told me were.'

'Well, that's no surprise. Gran's always been special. So what happened? Between you and Aaron, I mean.'

'It became too difficult. I never knew when I could be free. And then... as she deteriorated... I couldn't go off out enjoying myself when she might be wandering the streets, or burning the house down.'

'So you let him go.'

'You can't string people along.'

'But Gran doesn't need you now. Not full time at least. Does he know?'

'You can't ring somebody out of the blue and say, "I'm free; can we pick up where we left off?" Anyway, he's probably married by now.'

'Or he might just be lonely and missing you.'

'Have you spoken to Pandora recently?'

'Not for a few weeks. Why?'

'Something's not right. She *says* they're all fine but...'

'You worry too much. You ought to be out there having a wonderful new life with your Mr Wiseman...'

'I wish I'd never told you.'

'...instead of imagining all the things that could be going wrong for everyone else. You've got enough on your plate with Gran. Pandora's OK.'

'Well, for the record, Gran was in great form, today. She actually made me laugh.'

I smile, remembering. It's becoming easier to see the funny side. Affection is creeping back in.

Mother was sitting dozing when I arrived. I watched her for 20 minutes. She looks so reduced. Her scalp showing through her hair, her arms so thin. Her fingers are perpetually restless, even in sleep. But her nails are long, beautifully shaped, polished in *Frosted Pearl* by the lady who comes in twice a month to provide 'pampering'. Mother never wore nail polish in her mentally competent days. And, aged 16, I well remember hiding my hands inside my sleeves, the first time I tried it out.

The kitchen assistant woke her, barging in after the most cursory of knocks.

'Sorry! Did I wake you, sweetheart? Me and me big trolley. It's coffee-time... here we are. Nice an' milky, like you like it. One sugar. Not too hot. Watch yourself, mind. And how about a nice wee custard cream? Your favourite, eh? Coffee for you too, dear?'

I accepted the tasteless brew and she trundled off down the corridor.

Mother sat bleary-eyed, staring at the cup. Since when did she take sugar in her coffee? Or lots of milk, come to that? And she always loathed custard creams.

I leaned over and said quietly, 'I'm here, Mother. Jessica. Your daughter.'

'Where's George?'

'He's been waiting a long time for you. Won't he be chuffed to see you when you eventually decide to pay him a visit? Wonder what he'll say when he sees you. "Did I invite you?" maybe. You'll feel right at home.'

'Don't be daft,' she said.

I hugged her.

After James has gone home to Margot, I daub a test-splodge of the new emulsion on the bare plaster. Yes, I like it. It's the right colour for this room. Neutral. Unlike the war-zone Adeline and I created, until I reached my teens and she moved out. I became fiercely protective of my territory and I still remember the sense of betrayal when I returned home after my second term at university to find the ornaments changed and two of the drawers commandeered for table linen. Now, four decades later, I wonder: was it the same for my mother when I started to claim parts of her home? What must it have felt like to have her own child turn jailor?

I must hold onto this thought next time she makes me wish she was dead.

Chapter 3

I PAUSE FOR a long moment before entering Mother's old bedroom. As children we knew it was off limits; as I grew older I understood.

The crush in her wardrobes comes as no surprise. Twice before I've had to select clothes from these racks: first when I wrenched her away to live in my home, then when she went into The Morningside. But before that, countless times, I've dashed in, seizing something – anything – to replace a soiled, burned, shredded or lost garment.

The wardrobes are mahogany and vast, with scrollery and castle-sized keyholes. I can only marvel that one tiny woman could compress so many boxes and bags into this space. I find spangled shoes stuffed inside Wellington boots, a baby's bootee inside a handbag. Seamed silk stockings tangle with a book about wartime economies. A strip of Belgian lace snags on a paper of snap fasteners. A nightdress I gave her, still in its wrapping, is stained with something dark and sticky. Embroidery kits hide between used sheets.

Everything on hangers seems more manageable. I scribble four labels: 'The Morningside'; 'Alter'… hmm, she has lost so much weight over the last few years, dare I attempt such a task? 'Charity shops'; 'Recycling'.

A lavender-blue silk dress drags me back to my childhood.

Mother twirling under the light, the soft drapes floating about her, her look coquettish as Father says, with something odd in his voice, 'Is that a new frock, Doris?' It was such a rare thing for them to go out together that I lay in bed convinced they would meet with an accident on the way home, and we children would be orphans. I never saw Mother in that dress again. It's too beautiful to dispose of. I sneak it into the collection for going back to my house.

A grey tailored suit, the cut exceptional. My sharpest memory is of Mother wearing it when she stopped wearing black. For her son. I abandon it to the designer rail of some charity shop.

Good grief! What on earth is a man's kilt doing here? The genuine article, eight yards of tartan, beautifully finished. Weighs a ton. Surely Mother couldn't have smuggled this out of a shop unseen? But then, I never ceased to be amazed at the stream of things she managed to appropriate without being caught. At first I returned the magazines and sweeties and perfume and jewellery with abject apologies. Then I took to slipping things back without reporting their absence: electrical goods, silk scarves, books. Latterly I gave James items to take to an Oxfam shop on the other side of town. Mother had become a kind of modern-day Robin Hood and I her henchman. But a perfect kilt? It must be worth a mint. I will return it myself.

Oh, here's the suit Mother wore to Pandora's wedding. Pale pink linen. Fitted jacket, slim skirt. Matching sculpted pink hat. Pandora chose it. Just as she insisted I wear mauve silk. To 'complement the wedding party'. Mauve! With my skin!

Her father, Lewis, absolutely refused to wear what he called a 'penguin suit'. The desperate bride tried every wile in her repertoire, including hiring the whole outfit, but no, he stands out in the wedding pictures as the only one in a lounge suit. Nothing in Pandora's smile betrays her anguish. Nowadays she'd probably have asked the photographer to digitally eliminate the evidence of his non-compliance, but her wedding pre-dated such facilities. That suit remains as a testament to her persistent disappointment in us.

The groom, Enrico, looks sheepish; his father, bewildered. So perhaps Lewis had a point. And I envied him his courage as I donned the mauve and watched the colour drain from my face. But in fairness, Mother's pink suited her to perfection. The stain of a strawberry on the sleeve is still there. She probably never wore the outfit again. Perhaps the clouds had already begun to obscure her memory. Who knows how long she covered her forgetfulness before I started to suspect?

The cornflower-blue ensemble she wore to James' wedding is looking much sadder. Her own choice, based on a lifetime's understanding of what became her. It's worn state marks it out as a loved friend, fit now only for the recycling bag.

I shake out the claret dress she bought for James' graduation. How proud she was of his achievement, how devastated that he could obtain only three tickets and she could not attend. We gave her an enlarged photo, which she displayed with pride, but I never saw her in that red dress without a pang of guilt.

She was wearing red when I went to visit her yesterday afternoon. This same deep crimson, but synthetic, not merino wool. By the time she'd spilled her hot milk and brushed against the pollen of the lilies 'that prime minister' had brought her, it had survived for less than two hours. I want to swathe her in aprons but the staff just whip things off and throw them in the laundry. Who am I to interfere?

Most of the garments in Mother's wardrobes hold no sentiment for me so I sort them swiftly according to size and condition. Until, that is, I come to a dark green outfit with a box-pleat skirt. I had no idea she still had it.

I close my eyes and sink down onto the bed, clutching the suit, my own wedding swirling across my vision. Mother twittering round me like some forest elf; Adeline wailing about the tightness of her bridesmaid's dress after her holiday in Spain; Father walking in a measured stride beside me as if on parade. And me, a curious sense of detachment beneath the boned satin.

I slip my arms into the jacket, turn this way and that, remembering. I zip the skirt, leaving the waistband unbuttoned, the loose pleats accommodating my broader hips. It looks surprisingly neat. How did Mother feel that day? In the mirror, her motherhood merges with mine. The suit joins the pile for going to my home. The thoughts need time.

Many of these items are clearly brand new mail order 'bargains', neither Mother's size nor style. By the time I've emptied the racks I have a row of carrier bags to go to charity. James will remove those tonight, before I can change my mind. The smaller piles destined for The Morningside or my house I carry down and stow in the boot of my car, my dubious reasons safe from questioning.

Once I've closed those massive wardrobe doors, the room looks much the same, a denial of my emotional day. I shroud the furniture in old sheets. It will be steadier than ladders to stand on while I paint. Another phase in its long life.

What a lot it has witnessed.

Doris as a young wife, excited by ownership of her first home, is a mystery figure to me. My earliest memories of my parents are of two people whose world centred on their family. Hard to imagine them before we existed. Doris and George. Just the two of them.

Easier to picture Mother pregnant. I was born barely a year after their wedding. (Although there are no photos. 'People didn't flaunt their bumps in those days. And besides, we didn't even own a camera when we got married.') Then Adeline and Eugene at two-year intervals, and Lionel six years later. I always wondered if he was 'a mistake'. Maybe she loved him so fiercely in order to compensate.

As newborns we all lay in the family cot on Mother's side of the mahogany bed, within easy reach when we woke. 'You didn't cry much, any of you,' she used to say. 'You knew your food was coming. Every three hours for the first week or so, then every four hours. No demand feeding in those days. Routine, that's what babies need. Routine and security.'

How different from her granddaughter's approach. 'There's no way I'm going to let this baby rule my life. It'll be in its own room from the start. And bottle-fed. I'm not ruining *my* figure.'

Family life matters to me. Perhaps that's why my internal pictures of Doris the young parent are the ones I've clung to as she slipped away from me. The stories she invented, the games, the sewing, crafting, baking. By the time Adeline came along Father had invested in a Brownie box camera. A bookshelf full of albums – meticulously arranged in chronological order and invaluable aids as the plaque started to invade Mother's brain – holds a record of our holidays, home-life, schooldays, outdated clothes and stilted poses.

Doris as a new widow, alone in this big bed, that I don't want to picture. It brings my own loss too close for comfort.

But Mother's restless search for George now seems to me to reflect the enormity of her loneliness. Is the man she seeks the same one I remember? In my mind he remains a rather remote figure. Placid, bookish, given to flashes of paternal affection.

The annual excursion to the forest to select a Christmas tree. The chocolate darkness, the scent of cut wood, the pyramid of festivity Mother made from the seven feet of Douglas Fir he dragged home.

The tree-house, constructed entirely without our prior knowledge. The bounce of the planks under our feet; the held breath hiding from the neighbourhood children lest they devalue this labour of love.

The seaside chalet in Devon, big enough for 10. Father organising games on the beach, swimming with us in the sea, buying in food that made Mother gasp: shrimps and asparagus, marinated steaks, chocolate brazils. Hushing us as Mum actually dozed on the veranda, her knitting slipping from her fingers, while we stifled giggles.

The night when he found me weeping in the back garden.

'What on earth's the matter, Jessica? You'll catch your death of cold out here.'

'I don't care.'

'Don't be silly. Of course you care.'

'I do not!'

'Why? What's wrong?'

'I know I don't belong.'

'Belong where?'

'In this family.'

I'd done it this time. His voice came out all starched as if he needed something stiff to hold in his annoyance.

'Why on earth would you think that?'

'I don't look like you or Mum.'

'Rubbish. You have your mother's build. And you're the spitting image of your grandmother on her side – and you're every bit as stubborn as she was!'

'But Adeline looks exactly like you.'

'I hope for her sake she doesn't!' he said with a lopsided grin.

'And the boys – they've got your hair and your nose and Lionel's got Mum's eyes. The others are all tall.'

'And you're petite, like Mum. You have your grandmother's curls. What brought all this on?'

'Nesta. At school. She says her mum reckons I'm not a real Mannering.'

'And what would Nesta's mother know about anything – whoever she is? You mustn't take any notice of what spiteful little girls say. Who is this Nesta anyway?'

'She's got sticky-out teeth and d'you know, Dad, she can't even do algebra. I mean, how can anybody not see how to do easy-peasy stuff like *algebra*?'

'There's your answer. She's jealous. Now come on, girl, stir your stumps. I'm freezing out here. A nice hot cup of tea is what we both need and no more of this silly nonsense.'

And my reliably undemonstrative father gave me a swift hug.

I know that Mother taught me far more, mopped up more tears, coaxed me out of more fancied slights, laid down far more stepping stones to adulthood, but somehow Father's rare excursions into her realm had a more memorable impact on me.

When it was my turn to face a daughter's angst about her appearance, I remembered his patience and listened to Pandora's fears with sympathy.

Being the first of his offspring to reach adolescence, I probably tested my father's boundaries more than I realised, but my abiding memory is of a disciplined man, slow to anger, who taught by example, and I for one, suffered more from his disappointment in me than from any verbal reproof.

I was 29 when he died. He was only 53.

Nothing prepares you for news like that. Mother's voice was flat as she told me over the phone. It was a massive heart attack. He'd been walking up the stairs at the wool mill he managed, a journey he'd made thousands of times. The steps were no steeper that day, the day no more stressful than usual. In his bag he had the yearly budget to work on, but it was no more onerous than it had been every other year. Why had his heart failed the test on that particular day?

I went home immediately. Mother allowed me to accompany her to the undertaker, to the manse, to the solicitor, but I was superfluous to requirements. She was totally in control of everything.

But the shock of Dad's death was totally eclipsed 15 years later by the loss of my brother, Lionel.

He was 32. Just 32.

It was this tragedy that changed Mother. Something in her died with him and I came to dread the closed expression that told me she had gone somewhere I couldn't follow. But after a few years my sympathy edged into resentment. Her withdrawal seemed selfish, it denied our grief. I wished I could have talked to my father about it, he would have understood.

I sometimes wonder, could the shock of Lionel's death have started her dementia? Is such a thing medically possible? The loss of her identity and the endless searching do seem to mirror profound maternal sorrow. Surely, I told myself, this survivor could not *now* fragment inside. And since she continued to conjure up her habitual graciousness for visitors, and provide excuses for her lapses, she made me doubt my early suspicions.

James takes the stairs two at a time and the warmth of his presence banishes my melancholy.

'I popped in to see Gran at lunchtime today. She was dozing most of the time but she's looking good.'

'I agree, she looks much less strained than she did.'

'She sent me off to find Charles Darwin to sort out the plumbing, which she reckons has been tinkered with by the Poles.'

I give him a watery smile.

'And what about you?' he says briskly. 'We need to plump *you* up now.'

'No thank you! I need to *lose* a few pounds, not put anything on.'

'The rate you're working, you'll be skin and bone by the time this place goes on the market. You really must ease up, Mum.'

'I will, dear. Just as soon as this is all finished.'

I don't tell him that I've agreed to have Pandora's children for two weeks in the summer, while she goes on holiday to Italy – I presume with Enrico. Her brittle tone doesn't suggest lazy days or companionship. James has enough worries of his own with the new mortgage and the boys. Is Aunt Beatrice right? Would Mother prefer the money from this house to go to helping her grandchildren?

He's looking at me quizzically.

'What?' I say. It sounds sharp. I soften it with a smile.

'You were miles away.'

'Sorry.'

'Oh, before I forget, I cut this out of the paper yesterday.' He hands me a torn cutting.

I read it in silence. Sedatives – chemical coshes, it actually says – to keep them calm and manageable, are apparently killing people with Alzheimer's prematurely. About 23,000 a year.

'Remember that family at The Morningside?' James says. 'The ones that moved their grandad there from that other home? Died a few months ago.'

'The Sullivans?'

'That's the ones. They reckoned *he* was being doped to keep him quiet, didn't they?'

'They also reckoned the staff were cruel to him. Nice enough when they were there, but shouting at him and ignoring him when they weren't. Dumping a tray beside him at mealtimes, knowing he couldn't feed himself. That's why they moved him to The Morningside. But they were pretty paranoid.'

James looks at me strangely.

'What?' I say.

'You don't believe them?'

'I don't know. But it's no picnic looking after a whole pile of dementing people, you know. You can't believe everything they say. Gran used to accuse me of hurting her. Maybe he *thought* they were shouting at him but actually...'

He shrugs.

'Horrible as it is, I'm afraid the Sullivans are probably telling the truth. I didn't say anything – didn't want to worry you. But I did a bit of digging, and that home Mr Sullivan came from... there've been some complaints. The manager and one of the senior staff left in a bit of a hurry a couple of months ago. There's an investigation going on.'

'Oh dear.' I feel sick. I know it happens. But I knew Mr Sullivan. I know his daughter.

'Of course, bullying, maltreatment, that's a different thing from this,' I say, flicking the newspaper cutting.

'I know. But these drugs, it says they shorten life.'

I shrug. 'Maybe that's a good thing.'
'Mother!'
'Who wants to prolong a living death?'
'It's an abuse of human rights.'
'So's dementia.'

Chapter 4

WOULD MOTHER BE better off dead?

The phone startles me. It's my uncle.

'I thought I'd ring to see if Doris is any better.'

'She's much the same, Uncle Syd.'

'Will you tell her I rang?'

'Course I will.'

'She was always the strong one, our Doris. Kept the rest of us in order.'

'I can believe that!'

'It shouldn't have happened to her. Not after all she did.'

'Nobody deserves it.'

'Her least of all.'

'They're taking good care of her. The home's lovely. And she gets out into the garden. I think she enjoys the roses.'

'Doris was always keen on the garden. I'm glad she's still got that. And there's enough money, Jess? I can send a bit if you need it.'

'That's sweet of you, but no, we're fine. Once the house is sold, there'll be plenty.'

By the time he's finished his limited repertoire of conversation pieces, the tub of Polyfilla has set rigid.

'Uncle Syd.'

'Yes.'

'D'you remember a girl called Cissy Clarendon? In Beatrice's year at school.'

'Can't say I do.'

'It doesn't matter.'

Now I'm prepared for the real thing.

Aunt Beatrice listens to my report on her sister's state of health giving her usual perfunctory responses. She's in automatic mode and I drop the question without preamble.

'D'you remember a girl called Cissy Clarendon? She was in your class at school.'

Silence.

'Aunt Beatrice?'

'Vaguely. Why?'

'I met one of her relations a while back. Apparently she remembers you. And Mum.'

'Don't pay attention to gossip, Jessica. Girls can be petty. Cissy was always jealous of me.'

'Jealous? Why?'

'Who knows? Because I was prettier? Because the boys liked me? I don't know.'

'She had a high opinion of Mum, apparently. That's nice to know, isn't it? Even though they were only schoolgirls.'

'Doris wasn't the competition.'

'What d'you remember about her – Cissy, I mean?'

'Nothing much. She was brainy. Always won prizes. Two left feet though. Hopeless at games.'

'Oh.'

'I was in the athletics team and the hockey team.'

'I see.'

'What relative of hers did you meet?'

'Her son.'

'So she had a kid then.' And under her breath, 'The hypocrite.'

'You've lost me, Aunt Beatrice.'

'It's nothing. Give my love to your mother when you see her.

I will try to get up, only things are so hectic down here.'

I get back to the third bedroom – the oddest shape with its slopes and angles. Scant furniture and an alien smell. This was Eugene and Lionel's old room, the scene of physical fights and outright hostility at times, but never the sulks and backbiting we girls indulged in.

I'm leaving in the stud partition Dad added to give the boys privacy. Separation looks better on the agent's specification: *On the first floor, bathroom and four spacious bedrooms.*

It has taken three evenings to clear out the clutter Mother accumulated in here, everything from lumps of coal to a coffee table I've never seen before. I tremble to think how she acquired a lot of the stuff, but I know exactly why the cover on the bed has a hole cut out of the middle ('*A moth got trapped in the cloth. I had to set it free.*'); how the radiator acquired that dent ('*George keeps singing in there – all night long. He keeps me awake.*'); and where the partner of the horse's-head bookend went ('*Lionel's frightened of horses. And monsters. Dear Lionel. He's my youngest, you know.*').

The echo of her words brings a surge of sorrow. It's in this room that Lionel is most alive to me. I can see him yet, aged about nine, newly woken, his hair sticking up like an exclamation mark, his pyjama jacket buttoned wrongly, indignation in every line.

'Go away, Jessica. Girls can't come in here.'

Or, a mere three years later, huddling in the dark of his room, shivering in the cold, while he breathlessly reported the success of his first date with Sadie Ransome. Being 10 years older I was deemed sufficiently au fait with the ways of the world to be both confidante and agony aunt.

Emptied, the rooms echo to my movements.

As I roller the walls, the teenage Eugene seems to watch me painting him out of the picture. How different his life is now. Since he settled in Australia he has prospered, acquired an elegant home and an artistic wife. There is no place for ancient relics in his life, not even the prized Lego, never mind Mother.

Strange how the choice of a partner can change the course of history. Jane converted Eugene from a globe-trotting sailor with uncompromising socialist beliefs into a conventional businessman with a mortgage and three daughters.

Percy gave Adeline no offspring but left her with a chip on her shoulder. Ferdie followed and increased the size of the chip in his brief reign, but also gave her a heightened taste for the high-life, which she has continued to cultivate, thanks to his generous alimony.

Lionel didn't live long enough to find anyone to clip his adventurous wings.

And Lewis reduced my horizons to... No, it would be too disloyal and too simplistic to attribute my limited aspirations to his influence. And yet Eugene, Adeline and I grew up under the same regime with the same strong woman inculcating our values and morals, the same quiet man setting our example. Curious. And sobering.

What did Mother make of our choices, I wonder? She never said. And now I'll never know.

Is my brain slowing too? When did I start to notice things weren't right with Mother?

She started muddling names and facts. Don't all women have lapses of concentration as they reach a certain age?

She spoke of Lionel in the present tense. I assumed that she meant Eugene, or that she was lost in her own memories.

She told me of impossible things she'd done at the weekend. She must have meant Thursday.

She maintained I hadn't informed her of something. I presumed I'd actually been too busy to tell her.

And she became a past master at covering up her errors. I had to admire her skill. I can see Aunt Beatrice's face now.

'Doris, that's the second time you've mentioned Mamma. She's dead. She died donkey's years ago.'

'I know that. I'm not stupid.'

'Well, why d'you keep speaking about these people as if they're still here?'

'To check if you're even half listening.'

It was more frustrating with the GP. Mother's charm and quick thinking gave the lie to my misgivings.

It was a crumpled letter in the kitchen bin that alerted me to her financial difficulties. The official heading of the bank caught my attention. Would Mrs Mannering come in to discuss 'various discrepancies'.

Mother was sitting at the dining table leafing through a catalogue for tailor-made shoes at the time. When I spoke she snapped it shut, looking at once guilty and defiant.

'Jessica! Why do you creep up on people like that?'

'Sorry. Mum, this letter was in your bin. I couldn't help but notice who it's from. Is everything all right?'

'Yes, of course it is. Why wouldn't it be? And since when did it become acceptable for people to poke about in other people's private correspondence?'

'Honestly, I wasn't poking...' Her look was more eloquent than words. 'I'm sorry, but you would tell me if you had money troubles?'

'There's nothing to tell.'

She'd always been so competent with financial matters and something of that expertise covered her tracks. Some of the evidence I'm only now finding. Goods purchased from catalogues, hidden in cupboards. Bank statements, cash, final demands, stuffed into improbable places. Was she sufficiently aware to be alarmed by them? Was she conscious of giving her bank details to unauthorised people? I can only hope not. At the time I was comforted by her robust denials. I *wanted* there to be nothing amiss. Leaving me free for Aaron.

There was no consolation in having my suspicions confirmed. Once I'd finally accepted what was happening... after Aaron... the decline seemed to escalate. She lost the capacity to cook, to dress herself, to attend to her own hygiene.

The change in her personality was hardest. I kept telling myself it was the disease that generated her restlessness and aggression, but it didn't ease the daily battle. She dragged my standards down as well as her own and I could only try to be glad that she was unaware of the degradation. Or so I thought. But now...

As I unpack the signs of her lonely struggle hovering between two worlds, I regret colluding with her pretence, denying her comfort when she most needed it. And where else could this feisty woman turn for support? Not professional avenues certainly. With her there was only ever her best side.

The phone startles me into dropping the roller, leaving a slur of emulsion across the floorboards. I curse under my breath.

Aunt Beatrice makes no effort to hide her resentment. 'I thought you must be out. I was about to ring off.'

'I was painting.'

'Well anyway, I've had an idea. Electronic tagging. I heard about it on the radio. That would make a difference, wouldn't it?'

'Make a difference to what?'

'To Doris.'

I take a deep breath. 'I can't believe the home would agree to tag a lady who's suffering from Alzheimer's.'

'No, not the *home*! If she was tagged, she wouldn't need to be there. Then when she wandered off, you'd be able to find her.'

'Aunt Beatrice, I'm sure you mean well.' Liar! 'But Mum is in The Morningside to stay. She's not coming out, with or without a tag.'

'But then you wouldn't need to sell her house. You'd be better off,' Beatrice wheedles.

'No, I wouldn't. I'm beginning to realise what it's taken out of me, caring for her all those years. I can't do it again. I can't.'

'Did you ever consider tagging?'

'Strangely enough, no, I didn't.'

'There you are then. You weren't in possession of all the facts.'

'You misunderstand me. I *know* about tagging. For criminals and offenders. Not for *my mother*.'

'It's only like keeping tabs on pets. So they're safe. People return them if they get lost.'

'Mother is not a pet. And I have no intention of treating her like some Yorkshire terrier.'

'But remember all the times you were going out of your mind because you didn't know where she was.'

'Oh, believe me, I remember. But tagging isn't the answer.'

'And locking her up in a home is?' Aunt Beatrice says sharply. 'Selling her house?'

I grit my teeth as she ploughs on.

'Nowadays parents track their kids with mobile phones. It's all the rage. It's the same thing. You want to know they're safe. We could keep track of Doris and let her do what she wants to do. You know, she might be better – not so frustrated and upset if she had her freedom back. She'd feel more in control.'

'I can see you've been giving this a lot of thought and you said "we", so I take it you would have her part of the time, to give her this happy second chance.'

'Oh no! London's no place for somebody like Doris.'

'Have you talked about it to Adeline? Is she going to take a turn?'

'No, I haven't.'

'And she could pop over to Melbourne, to Eugene – maybe in the wintertime, so she has year-round summers.'

'Now you're being silly.' Aunt Beatrice sounds sulky.

'Realistic, I think you'll find. Mother is past being looked after by any of us, we have to accept that. And the house *is* going on the market. Probably in September. Now if you'll excuse me, I really must get back to the painting before the roller dries out completely.'

Does she ever wonder whether she has inherited the same

gene? I do. I might be doubly prone to it, in fact. Father died too young to know.

Try as I will I can't eradicate the conversation from my mind as I resume painting. For I too had scratched around for ways of keeping Mother out of institutions – although for very different reasons.

I appealed to doctors...

'Mrs Burden, there aren't the funds to buy the drugs you think would help your mother. Some trusts do find the money but unfortunately this one can't.'

It was only £2.50 a day. That's what I was asking for. For a drug that could potentially slow this horrendous disease. A mere £2.50. The price of a large bag of potatoes. Or six quality sausages. Or a packet of pea seeds.

I applied to politicians...

Dear Mrs Burden

We are sorry you see this as cost-cutting. The trust for your area seems to have taken on board the advice given by NICE – the National Institute for Health and Clinical Excellence – an independent organisation appointed to provide guidance on the promotion of good health and the prevention and treatment of ill health. Based on expertise within the healthcare community as well as the academic world, NICE has assessed the drug you mention, Aricept, as not giving sufficient improvement to be appropriate in the early stages of Alzheimer's Disease. We suggest that you speak to your GP about extra help from the social services in your area.

I know Scotland isn't answerable to NICE but the iniquity of postcode lotteries made me furious. I let my GP have it, both barrels. He was defensive.

'Bodies like NICE have a difficult job. Whatever they do they get criticised. This isn't an arbitrary decision based on personal whim or individual preference. They're trying to juggle fairness with sound economics.'

'Explain to me how it's fair.'

'In general, NICE approves drugs that cost less than £20,000 for every extra year of improved quality of life. Above £30,000 the drug is usually turned down. In between they need to be persuaded of the benefits.'

'Has there been any debate about the financial ceilings they impose?' I raged.

'Well, no.'

'Who says that's all that should be available? Not families of people with dementia, I bet!'

Pandora became an unexpected ally. Her friend's father had been given Aricept early on. It gave him a whole new lease of life. He'd used the time to set his affairs in order and establish a proper plan so the family could respect his wishes when he could no longer state them competently himself. *That* GP, according to Pandora, had a relative with Alzheimer's. He fought for his patients. He told them outright they shouldn't pay for the drugs or they'd end up paying for everything.

Pandora's comments sent me searching. The letters were fierce. The NHS should be free at the point of delivery, 'fair and equitable for all', said somebody from the BMA. Once you let NHS patients pay for extra treatment, you risk tempting future governments to cut the number of drugs they fund.

NICE is 'bureaucratic, unaccountable and run by economists not doctors', stormed the Patients' Association. The decision was 'unreasonable and cruel'. 'What about the Hippocratic pledge to do no harm?' asked a Dr Thain of Tavistock. 'This decision smacks of a principle of equal unfairness: don't do a good turn for anyone in case you have to do it for everyone.'

Once I was alerted to the inequality I started seeing it everywhere. Primary Care Trusts refusing to honour consultants' prescriptions. People dying prematurely because of shortfalls in funding for life-prolonging drugs. The better-off or more determined patients (and their aged parents) spending their pension funds and savings buying a little more time to see a grandchild, to celebrate one more anniversary, say a proper goodbye.

I begged social workers for better community support and respite care.

'*We have many families who need support and limited resources so we must prioritise need. We can assure you that your case is being viewed with sympathy and we will monitor the situation with care*,' I was told.

That would be monitoring by remote control, then. I certainly never took part in any kind of assessment.

I even sank to offering myself to a BBC reporter as someone willing to describe our situation on TV, if it would pressure the authorities into providing the resources we needed. In the end they chose a retired army colonel who'd cared for his wife devotedly for 25 years and vowed never to relinquish her care to another living soul as long as he lived. I had to switch off. A saint was exactly the kind of person I did *not* need.

And now, here I am, being made to feel guilty all over again.

I'd like to tag Aunt Beatrice!

Chapter 5

SORTING THE HOUSE is bound to bring back memories, but last night's blast from the past was of a different order.

The message was waiting for me on the answerphone.

'Hello, Jessica. This is Aaron. Aaron Wiseman. I'm up here visiting relations and wondered if you were available, maybe for a coffee? For old times' sake.'

He hoped I was free.

Free? Free of what? For what?

I need hard work. I'll get started on the sitting room.

Just holding the brochures about homes for people with dementia is painful. We rated them, James and I together, then visited those within a thirty-mile radius that scored four or five stars. There were only three.

No competition. The Morningside won five stars from the outset. Person-centred care was their watchword. Space, flexibility, privacy, respect, realising full potential – bespoke caring, writ large. The welcome we'd received there clinched it. And the views from what would be Mother's room. If you *had* to put your relative behind locked doors this was the door you'd choose, if you could afford it. Even James gulped when he saw the prices, but he recovered immediately.

'It'll be worth every penny to have peace of mind.'

'And it's her money,' I said.

I toss the brochures into the recycling bag. It's done. There's no going back.

'*I hope you're free.*'

Just hearing Aaron's voice... I give myself a mental shake. Get a grip! Don't read something into nothing.

Glasses, china, vases, bubble-wrapped and packed into the boxes James left in the hall. There's only one set of champagne flutes I intend to keep for myself, bought for her 70th birthday. Expensive, beautiful and, I suspect, never used.

Why did he ring?

I stack pictures back-to-back and think of the gems uncovered on *Antiques Roadshow*. Maybe I could consult Aaron. Paintings were one of his passions. It would be an excuse... *No!* If someone somewhere finds a treasure, good luck to them.

All the rooms have cupboards built into the walls, and for as long as I can remember, the bottom section in the sitting-room recess has housed Mother's collection of Christmas decorations. Most of the familiar things are still there, but in her recent squirrellings she's added a couple of magazines, an electricity bill, a leaking biro, a Brownie camera, sweets, old coins, about a hundred second-class postage stamps – the fact that they're a special Christmas issue gives her action authenticity. I like to think her brain registered the connection.

I trickle the tinsel through my hands, seeing her darting hither and thither creating a wonderland for her children out of the same strands and balls, year after year. I salvage two lengths of tinsel, a box of glass baubles, and the all-important glittery ball which always hung from the centre light. Maybe they will strike a chord in her memory if I put them up in her room... the first year she won't be with the family.

I can't bear it. I turn too abruptly and stub my foot against the TV stand. At least now I have a legitimate explanation for the tears. I slump down onto the settee, nursing the injury. Mother is there, sitting beside me. Not so very long ago. Watching TV was one of the last companionable things we could share. She loved costume dramas and medical soaps and anything starring Judi Dench. *Keeping up Appearances* made her laugh even on the umpteenth re-run. Seeing them in this room gave the experience added spice. For this was our 'special occasion' room. Most of the year it was austere, kept ready for unexpected visitors, but when birthdays, Easter, Christmas and the New Year came, Mother transformed it. And we could romp to our hearts' content.

But I must press on.

Seven photo albums stack the shelves in the window.

The first one I open brings a welter of mixed emotions. Especially today, now that Aaron has been in touch.

Lewis was a handsome groom, towering over me by 10 inches, neat, tanned. I thought so then, when he was 26; I think so now.

I was already established, teaching English, when Mr Burden came to give lessons on the oboe to a handful of pupils. He was a gifted soloist, less successful with children. He occasionally sought refuge in the staff room while he waited for his next student to arrive and I took pity on his shyness.

Conversation with Lewis was hard work, but I saw it as a challenge. There *must* be more to this man. Gradually I learned that he was an only child whose parents died when he was in his teens. What must it be like to stand completely alone in the world? Who did he tell when he was successful, who shared his disappointments? Where did he go for Christmas?

He took me back to his cold bedsit and I saw for myself how few possessions he had.

He was slow in his reactions, gauche in his early attempts at affection. But I felt protective. I willed him to succeed.

The honeymoon was a disaster – well, for me.

Lewis had taken care of all the arrangements. He'd booked a room in a down-at-heel guesthouse in Brighton. On the fourth floor, no lifts, smelling of cigarette smoke, shared bathroom.

Twin beds with dubious stains on the mattresses and pillows. He wasted no time in pushing the beds together and stripping off his clothes. I saw him naked for the first time. The implications of his haste began to dawn on me when he climbed into bed, flung his leg over me, fumbled beneath my nightie and entered me with no foreplay of any kind. The pain made me clench my teeth. Afterwards, he thanked me, rolled over and went to sleep. I remember staring into the darkness contemplating a future devoid of finesse and conversation. I felt so alone. And there was no one I could tell.

The damage of that first attempt at intimacy (what a travesty of the word!) made every subsequent night of the honeymoon – and three mornings too – a misery for me. The innuendoes from the ancient waitress who doubled as chambermaid merely added to my doubt. Was there something wrong with me?

Once we had given Brighton Pavilion and the hardware shops a cursory look, Lewis wanted to spend the day dozing on the beach or strolling along the pier. The things I'd anticipated – the Regency architecture, the magnificent crescents and squares, the arts scene – held no interest for him. Nothing tempted him to explore beyond the narrow road between the guesthouse and the sea. His contentment was a reproach. How could I want anything more than the company of my new husband?

I close the album and let the years soften the edges of my disappointment. For Lewis wasn't a cruel man. It was more that my imagination had different expectations.

The desire to understand the inner person wore thin over time and I sought intellectual stimulation elsewhere. Sex was another issue altogether, for I'd been breast-fed on the principles of chastity and faithfulness. During all our years of marriage it was always on Lewis' terms, always swift and silent.

But it's thanks to Lewis that I have my children. James reminds me of him most. And through him I've grown to appreciate Lewis' gentleness and patience. Father and son have shared the same ability to accept me exactly as I am – my terrier tendencies, my restlessness, my analytical approach to everything. I must take my share of responsibility for the fault-lines within our marriage.

I found a treasure for James today. 'You bought this for Gran when you were knee-high to a grasshopper. With your own money.'

He cradles the china wren in both hands. 'Winkled out of my piggy bank with a knife.'

'It was the very first time you went into a shop all on your own. Gran loved it. It was always in the front of her cabinet. It's a souvenir of how special you've always been to her.'

'Thanks, Mum. I think the kids might like to know that story. They won't ever know her as she really was.'

'Like the staff up at the home. To them she's simply a daft little biddy.'

He laughs with me and Lewis' deficiencies fade further into the past.

'Being here brings her back in a way,' James says softly.

'I know. But it's sad too, knowing she'll never come here again.'

'Mum, you did far more than most people would. She's lucky *you* are her daughter. Think of Davy Lockhart down the road; the way his daughters treated him. And there were *two* of them, but he was skin and bone, covered in sores and bruises, when the social services got in on the act.'

I shudder. 'Poor old Davy.'

'Gran had those sisters to tea once, didn't she? They were perfectly respectable ladies before the old man came to live with them. Before he drove them crazy. So don't beat yourself up.'

'I know, love. But it still hurts. Other families manage. Maybe I should have fought harder for extra help to keep her at home.'

'No guarantees there either. Grace Campbell, in the room next to Gran – her family spent a fortune buying in carers, but the old lady hated it, said they were unkind to her.'

'Maybe if I'd done things differently...'

'Maybe, maybe. Look. You tried. Nobody can do more than their best.'

'Well, you make sure you get hold of a hefty dose of rat poison as soon as I start showing signs!' I say.

He rolls his eyes. 'Which things did you find hardest to put up with?'

'The repetition. Definitely. The same question a million times.'

'Did I invite you?' he mimics, not unkindly.

'Squeaking her shoes together, flicking her nails, gnashing her teeth, scraping her spoon on her dish. Silly little things, but maddening when you have to listen to them over and over and over again.'

'It's a form of Chinese torture, that.'

'Enough to tip you over the edge into insanity, if you had time to stop and think about it. But, of course, she was always off again getting into some other scrape – usually something I hadn't even thought of taking precautions against. She was nothing if not inventive, your grandmother.'

'And you must admit, we've had our laughs too.'

I smile. 'Remember when she thought you were Nelson Mandela?'

'And that time Prince Philip was responsible for the Chinese kidnapping her daughter.'

'And when she maintained that Jesus had popped her knickers in the birdbath.'

He laughs. 'My favourite was when she marched off down the street in the altogether with a tea cosy on her head, and I met her and had to walk back with her because she flatly refused to get in the car – "that instrument of the Devil", she called it.'

I giggle. 'And she wouldn't let you cover her up with your jacket.'

'"Get that filthy rag away from me. Can't you see it's covered in fleas?"' He mimics her gestures as a well as her scandalised voice.

It's funny now. It wasn't then.

'So,' James says, giving me an arch look, 'make sure you're as amusing when you start to go doolally.' He glances at his watch. 'I need to watch the time today. Margot's going out, so I must get back for the kids.'

'You go, dear. I'll manage.'

'Don't be silly. You're already doing way too much. I see the skip came. I'll start chucking stuff into it in a mo but first, a cup of tea. I'm parched.'

He brings chocolate-coated shortbread biscuits in with it.

'Where did they come from?' I ask, leaning closer, suspicious in this house.

'They have not been nibbled, or dunked in pee, or been open for 10 months. I bought them in Sainsbury's on my way here. There you go. Sell-by date three months hence.'

'I shouldn't. My diet has gone totally to pot since I started on this house.'

'Rubbish! A sugar rush is exactly what the doctor orders.'

'Oh, I'm not talking about that kind of diet. I mean anti-oxidants and everything. To help prevent loads of things, not just Alzheimer's.'

'You sound just like Margot! Gorge on fruit, veg, pulses and fish. Lay off the dairy products, meat and alcohol. Stock up on blueberries and walnuts and seeds. Nothing about shortbread biscuits.'

'Well, no point in *inviting* trouble.'

'You think too much! You're as sane as anyone I know, and you *need* the energy from proper food. This is hard labour.'

'Well, maybe just the one then.'

I don't tell him that the very smell of shortbread makes me retch. My mother once did something unspeakable with it that will be forever etched on my senses... unless I too develop Alzheimer's.

Maybe there are advantages after all!

Not until we're busy again do I broach the subject uppermost in my mind.

'James, did you by any chance contact the man I told you about?'

'Which man?'

'Aaron Wiseman.'

'No. I've no idea where he lives.'

'Well, you might have found out. From the lawyer or something.'

'No. Why would I?'

'I just wondered.'

He stands stock still. 'Has he got in touch again?'

'Mm. That's why I thought...'

'And?'

'He left a message. That's all.'

'Saying?'

'He wants to meet for coffee.'

'And I hope you said, "Yes please, and can I bring my son along to vet your suitability".'

I can't help but smile.

'You *did* said yes, didn't you?' James' voice follows me as I leave the room.

'I haven't replied yet.'

'Mother! For goodness' sake!'

'I will. When I get the time.'

'Does he live locally then?'

'No. He's up visiting relatives.'

'Well, all the more reason to phone him straight away.'

Before I lock up that night I let my gaze wander over the architecture of my growing years. This room, that has been variations on the same theme since 1945, that houses the ghosts of family celebrations over six decades, will soon be a blank slate. A hint of eggshell blue on the walls, but mostly white.

As I close the door I fancy I see a fleeting figure scampering down the garden barefoot in the frost, her nightdress flapping round her knees. Running away for the umpteenth time. Running away was her specialist subject. Masterclass level!

Five times she escaped from the day centre, in spite of their so-called security. Three times she eluded the carer sent to give me a 'shopping break'. Now, I like to think her behaviour was one of the few expressions left for her native wit. Her brain *had* to be functioning logically to some extent to plan and execute such feats, and outwit her keepers.

In the end I changed the locks – on the garden gate as well as on the doors of the house. But that was after all the phone calls to say she was whizzing around on a roundabout at the local park at 2 a.m., or that she'd walked into some stranger's house, or hopped onto a bus to Berwick, or was shrieking blue murder in a police station.

It's been good remembering the happy times with James. But recalling her as she was, makes her present predicament the more poignant. Step by step she has sunk down into the basement of her being, and she will not return.

Aaron looks exactly as I remember him. I'm glad of a few moments before he looks up; the feelings are powerful.

And then he's striding towards me. I can't move.

He takes all the decisions I've agonised over out of my hands.

'Jessica! It is *so* lovely to see you again.' His hands around mine are firm. His lips touch each cheek for exactly long enough.

'And you.' I only need to receive.

He has chosen well – as he always did. The restaurant is discreet, our table apart without being too intimate.

He launches straight into enquiries about my mother and once he knows, I feel the weight slide from my shoulders. It's done. I don't ask if he's still single – but he reassures me anyway. From then on conversation is easy, we both know so much about each other. And this time there's no danger of any emergency to whisk me away.

He's in Edinburgh for four days. I truant from Mother's house for parts of every day and decline all offers of help with the renovations. I don't want this time tainted.

But he insists he wants to see Mother again.

It's peaceful visiting with him. He fields the repeated 'Did I invite you?' calmly and manages to turn the conversation to things that seem to hold her attention.

I drop in the question as he prepares to leave. 'Can I ask you one more thing?'

'Fire away.'

'According to my aunt, your mother and she didn't exactly get on. But you said that your mother had a huge admiration for my mother. Why? What did she do?'

'She was... kind and unselfish.'

I know he's prevaricating. 'I'd really like to know.'

There's a long pause.

'Please don't misconstrue this, but it's not mine to tell.'

'Aunt Beatrice wouldn't tell me, either,' I say. It sounds petulant and I instantly regret it.

He puts out a hand to touch my arm. There's something guarded in his eyes.

'Are *we* dependent on that old story?'

'No. Of course not. I just don't like to think there's anything... not quite right in the background.'

'There isn't. Not between you and me.'

Chapter 6

ALL THIS EMOTIONAL TURMOIL is making me ultra sensitive.

I hear warning bells even in Pandora's recorded message. *'Can you ring me, Mum?'*

She knows I'm working at her grandmother's house till late. Why didn't she ring me there? Is it too late to ring her back?

It isn't.

'Can you come over, Mum? I'm on my own this week. I could do with some company.'

'Is anything wrong?'

'No, but Karah's away at Brownie camp and there's just Max and me. It'd be great to have a good natter. Like old times.'

Before I realise it I've agreed to go over on Friday after she gets home from work – the evening I'd pencilled in for James to go through the papers from the box under the sideboard with me. But he'll understand. He knows I'm anxious about his sister. Perhaps on Friday I'll find out if I have reason to worry.

And it's the best week to go, as far as the house is concerned. It won't hold up progress. Because a 24-foot drop over the stairwell is not the place for a five foot two woman in her 60s. Last time the staircase was decorated Lewis did that corner, while I papered the bits I could reach with nothing more lethal than a stepladder. Standing on his tiptoes on a plank balanced between a ladder and a chair on the stair, one false move away from a broken leg, my husband grumbled, cursed and vowed never again. Time proved him to be right.

This time we'll pay someone else to take the risks. A local firm, recommended by a neighbour: *McCracken and Son. Friendly, efficient family business,* it said on the van.

'Give us a week, Mrs Burden. It's a scaffawdin' job. A week, 10 days max.'

I have low expectations. But soon the first-class bill for second-class workmanship will be forgotten in the flood of demands from the lawyers and estate agents and insurers and taxmen. And at least Mother will never know.

This has to be the easiest bit of the house to deal with from my point of view, a chance to slacken the pace for a few days. Every joint and muscle is crying out for a reprieve. There's only the hallstand to dispose of, three umbrellas and some coats. Then I have 'a week, 10 days max' to sort out the neglect in my own home. And spend the weekend with Aaron.

I'm unprepared for the wave of nostalgia when I take down the dark green raincoat. The picture of her tripping up the path to the washing line, the bird-table or the vegetable garden, burns against my eyelids. Always in that same green coat. For as far back as I can remember.

I inhale the musty odour but get no scent of her.

It's a weird feeling reaching into her pocket, somehow disrespectful of her privacy. There's a broken clothes peg, a tiny rounded stone, an embroidered handkerchief, a bus ticket stuck to a boiled sweet, a mangle of fluff, in the right pocket. I dump the lot straight in the bin.

I'm almost casual about delving into the left side.

The envelope looks unexceptional and I'm poised over the black sack ready to dispose of it when something stops me. The stamp is foreign, the postmark smudged out of existence. I draw out the single sheet of paper. The letterhead is a hospital in Pretoria. It's addressed to my grandparents.

The date is 1937.

Dear Mr and Mrs Fenton

It is with great sadness that I write to tell you that an unidentified male patient thought to be in his twenties was admitted to this hospital four months ago. He was unconscious on admission and suffering from a fever of unknown origin. Although we treated him aggressively I'm afraid we were unable to save him and he died without regaining consciousness during the night of 25th November.

Naturally the police made strenuous efforts to establish his identity in order to trace relatives. Last week a young gentleman came forward purporting to know the deceased whom he subsequently identified as your eldest son, Reuben. Documents were found in Reuben's flat which corroborate his friend's evidence and we are therefore writing to offer you our profound sympathy in your loss.

The police will, I'm sure, have contacted you to advise you of this sad news, but I thought you might like to hear from us that we did all in our power to try to save your son and regret that our efforts were in vain. It might be some small comfort to know that he did not suffer at any point while he was in our care, and indeed he was unaware that he was so gravely ill.

If you would like to receive further details of Reuben's illness and death please do not hesitate to contact us and we will do all in our power to satisfy your wishes in this regard.

Yours sincerely
Gilbert van Oosterhousen
Senior consultant in tropical medicine

Seven decades on that letter is still neatly folded in its envelope, as if its contents were known by heart. When did my mother start to carry this with her? Does it pre-date her illness and serve as evidence of her devotion to her big brother?

There was always a special tone in Mother's voice when she mentioned Reuben. He was her protector in childhood, her lodestar in adolescence, and her cherished memory in the decades that followed his death. Maybe tragedy endowed him with an aura of sainthood. Maybe he really was the hero she remembered. I shall never know.

Only once did I ever hear her mention her own pain.

The occasion was December 1981 – the beginning of the blackest weeks of my life. Forty-four years after Uncle Reuben died.

I had just buried my own beloved brother, Lionel. Mother had stood at the grave, a taut figure with clenched fists but parched eyes. I stood as close to her as I dared and watched numbly as the coffin slid through the drizzle and sank out of sight. I went through the motions of receiving condolences.

All three of us siblings were stunned by the sheer impertinence of death, but Eugene and I at least recognised our responsibility for Mother. I remember so distinctly how much like our father Eugene looked; aged at least a generation overnight, it seemed. Adeline, stunning in black, wandered around, silent and unresponsive.

It was that night, when Mother and I were left alone, here in this house – that it happened.

Keeping busy, I managed to retain my control for the first couple of hours after the guests had gone, but when my eye caught sight of a photograph of the four of us, the finality hit me foursquare. I fled upstairs and threw myself on the bed, muffling the sound of my agony in the covers. I couldn't rid myself of the horror: my brother left alone outside in the cold; all that soil, that heaviness suffocating him.

I don't know how long she'd been sitting on the edge of the bed, but when I felt her hand stroking my hair, I struggled to sit up. Her fingers pressed me back down.

'Cry, Jessica. Cry. Let it out.'

I flung myself on her chest and cried with an abandon I

had never experienced before, nor have since. She held me in silence.

'How can you be so calm, Mother? How *can* you?' I sobbed.

'There's more than one way to weep.'

'But he was your *son*!'

'And there can be no greater grief.'

I stared at her. This was *grief*?

'Pray God you will never know a pain like mine,' she said, so low I thought she was actually praying. 'But I know what you're feeling right now. I know, Jessica. I know.'

I looked up into her face and there was a look in her eyes that stilled my tongue.

'My brother Reuben died when he was only 23. All alone in a foreign country. He contracted some fever or other – we never knew what exactly. A stranger found him. It was months later we heard he was dead. He was never a letter-writer and we had no inkling that anything was amiss. For a long time I didn't believe it. I was only 17 at the time and I cherished a dream that the young man they found wasn't our Reuben; it was some other family's son. Reuben would breeze back into our lives and everything would be right again. I remember jumping up every time there was a knock at the door, thinking this would be him; actually waiting for the postman to bring that letter telling us he was having the time of his life somewhere exotic and far away. I remember searching crowds looking for a glimpse of him, imagining he'd lost his memory; we'd bring him home, coax him back to full strength again. I don't remember exactly what it was that finally extinguished my hope, but one thing I do know is that I thought then that I must die too. Life could not go on without him.'

I hardly dared to breathe. Her voice when it came again was all cracked at the edges.

'The guilt has never left me. And now... again...'

'But Mum!' I said, jerking upright, 'You couldn't have helped Uncle Reuben. It wasn't your fault. And there was no warning for Lionel. It was a massive brain haemorrhage. He died instantly. The post-mortem says so. He wouldn't have known a thing about it. Even if he'd been here and not in London there was nothing any of us could have done. They said that.'

She wasn't listening.

'He was always ambitious, Lionel. My baby. How could all that life, that energy, be wiped out? Snuffed out. Like a candle...'

That was the only time Mother and I ever cried together.

When Dad died, Mother kept her feelings under wraps. And I didn't weep for him as I had wept for my brother. It was natural that he would die before me, although no one expected him to go that young. But my kid brother had no business leaving me and I missed him in a million little ways.

I often looked at my mother and wondered at the emotion bottled up in her. I felt fear as well as awe, and perhaps an erosion of trust. If she could suppress a sorrow greater than mine, what else could she conceal? Could I ever believe what I saw again?

All the anger I see in her now, all the fear, is it the emotion finding expression at last? She's like a tree standing astride a great fault-line between the past and the future, her roots loosened by those seismic shocks, and with each reverberation she slips further into the crevasse.

And was it her habit of suppressing feeling that led to her loss of memory in the first place? Her grief was invisible, therefore it didn't exist. If her grief didn't exist, Lionel and Reuben didn't exist. And suddenly her whole life is in question. Does *she* exist?

And if tragedy could rob *my mother* of her sanity, what could losing a brother do to me, an altogether weaker character?

Of course, I haven't always viewed her plight with such sympathy. It's different now. But don't let me give the wrong impression. I've raged, I've rebelled, I've resented, I've hated.

Gross behaviour does that to you. The endless repetition does it. Enduring hostility, aggression, total lack of cooperation, hour after hour, day after day, week after week, only to have her answer the doctor's questions graciously, does it. Cleaning up after her, does it. Being nipped and hit and cursed, does it. Even the silences can do it.

Nowadays her moods are easier to handle because she's past retaining emotion. She's sure I'm a spy come to poison her – a doughnut will make her smile. She's afraid of the man in the TV who's watching her – brushing her hair takes her to a safe place. She's upset because her family have deserted her – we go into the garden and she's happy again. There's no longer any pressure to explain or reason with her.

I still wish she'd been given those drugs to slow the progress of the illness. I wish I'd found an advocate to plead for us. I resent the fact that families like ours still save the NHS millions but are denied support. But I no longer feel it was all my fault.

The remaining coats hanging in the hall, one grey, one black, hold no auras and give up no secrets. I drag the hallstand into the porch for James to take away.

The hall, stairwell and landing are ready for the professionals to emulsion over the memories.

Pandora is, as ever, immaculate. As is her house. There is no evidence that she's been at work all week, or that two children live here.

Max has already eaten when I arrive (I'm told) and soon afterwards he's despatched to his room to do 'homework for 90 minutes', 'music practice for 30', and then bed.

The take-away Turkish food which arrives soon after me is delicious. Pandora tells me about ingredients and traditions. I concentrate on not spilling anything.

Pandora never gives in to the craving for dessert. Ever. The coffee is so dark and strong my eyes water, but I sip it slowly, doing my best to follow the leaps of her conversation from the latest software, to the new neighbours 'from Kensington', Karah's school report, Pandora's own recent appraisal... like an express train.

'And Enrico? How's he?' I slip it in during a lull.

'He's fine. In Saudi Arabia this month.'

'He's away a lot,' I venture.

'It's the job.' Her hands are busy gathering the cups and saucers, her eyes watching her hands.

'Pandora, I don't want to interfere...'

'Then please don't,' she says briskly.

She suggests a stroll round the garden where Reg, her 'man', has clipped and swept and weeded until the lawns and borders look as if they're made out of modelling clay. Even the chairs on the patio are equidistant from each other around the table. I get the distinct impression that the birds circumvent the airspace above this precision.

'How's Gran's house coming on?' she asks, her first enquiry of the evening.

'We're getting there. Once the stairs are done, I'm going to tackle the dining room. It won't be as beautiful as yours, of course, but as long as it's freshened up – as long as it sells.'

'Would you fancy living there yourself?'

I'm taken aback and negotiate a water feature while I take my time answering.

'No. Too many memories. Besides, it's too big for one person. Would you ever want to move?'

'Probably not. I've got this place as I want it now. But *I* didn't do the work. You're doing Gran's house. It's your effort. It belongs to you. It's different.'

She bends down to feel the heavy head of a purple allium.

'Goodness, it's close tonight,' she says lightly. 'Feels like thunder in the air. I could do with a cold drink.'

Even in the gathering gloom she doesn't share confidences. Neither do I. And I dare not 'interfere'.

I go away more burdened than when I came.

Chapter 7

MOST OF THE FURNITURE in Mother's dining room is at least 90 years old. I've always loved the sideboard. It's solid oak and beautifully carved. I'd have it in my house if I had the space.

I feel the heat flood my neck and face. No! Such thoughts are the stuff of fantasy at my age.

It was Aaron who put the idea into my head. He can be too direct for comfort sometimes. But nowadays I need time – time to prepare for his thoughts. After our years apart there's so much mental work to be undone.

He made it clear from the outset. He's come up expressly to see me. He wants to pick up where we left off. And he has every intention of helping with Mother's house – no argument. 'Besides, it's the only way I'll get to see you!' Apparently I need saving from myself. James agrees.

I must admit Aaron's presence transforms the job. He works so cheerfully, as if it's the one place in the world he chooses to be. Together we achieve so much more and I can afford to take the evenings off – as he insists we do.

And he's been to The Morningside again. This time, however, Mother showed him exactly what dementia looks like, no holds barred. By the time we came out of the home, my fantasy had been reduced to ashes. I stumbled off towards the car. He caught up with me and made to touch my arm. I took a step away from him, holding out one hand to ward him off.

'Now you see why I can't let you...' I began before tears choked the words. 'I can't...'

He grasped my elbow and propelled me into the car.

'You, Jessica Burden, are coming for a good old-fashioned cup of tea.'

There were only two other customers in the café and, sitting outside in the sun on a quite unremarkable summer afternoon, I eventually stopped shaking. He didn't return to the subject of Mother until we'd finished one pot and ordered another one.

'OK,' he said, pushing his cup to one side and leaning forward on the table. 'Explain to me in words of one syllable why you can't let me get close to you.'

It was like a blow right between the eyes.

'You've seen what it's like.'

'I chose to. Remember?'

'Yes, but you weren't to know.'

He quirked an eyebrow. 'I'm not a kid. But that aside, why does knowing about your mother mean I must keep my distance from you?'

'Because... she *is* my mother. What if I went the same way?' There, it's said.

'What if *I* did?'

'That's different.'

'Oh? Why?'

I paused.

'Sounds to me like an excuse. But if you aren't interested...'

'You know it's not that.' It came out so quickly, before I had time to examine the implications. It seems to be catching.

'I *suspected,* but now I have confirmation, I am not going to let you escape a second time. Amongst my many foibles is stubbornness.'

The relief of having someone to talk to, someone who cares enough to listen, has become addictive. Even in so short a time.

I have this overwhelming need to make sure Aaron knows exactly what he's getting into. Urgently, before it's too hard to contemplate life without him. Again.

I find myself telling him about Pandora. About Blake. About Aunt Beatrice.

'But you know about her from your mother.'

'That was a long time ago, Jessica. A very long time ago. Before you and I were even born.'

'But...'

'But you're determined to show me how flawed your family are, huh?'

'Because you seem to have this distorted picture...'

'My picture is of you, not your family.'

'But your picture of me, that's distorted too.'

'Oh?'

'Yes. You only know half the story. OK, I chose to take care of Mum as long as I could, but I wasn't always nice to her.'

'Would anybody be, day in, day out?'

'And I rebelled inside – especially when you went away.'

'Ah, now that did hurt.'

'I'm sorry.' I can't go on.

'I don't hold it against you. I understood,' he says quietly. 'Much as I hated accepting your decision. And besides, I think I was largely to blame. I should have persisted.'

He reaches out and cups my face in his hands, searching my eyes for something. I can't dissemble, I don't know what he's looking for.

His kiss, that starts out so gently, is like no other kiss I've received before. 'You've no idea how much I've been wanting to do that,' he murmurs against my hair.

After what seems like forever, he turns my face up to his again.

'Would it bear repetition?'

Much later I try again to apologise for hurting him, but he puts his fingers against my lips.

'Let's forget about that and concentrate on getting it right this time. It wouldn't have been like this before. There was too much anxiety, too much guilt. On both sides. It's different now... isn't it?'

'Completely different.'

As he leaves that night a slow grin changes his expression.

'What are you thinking?'

'An unworthy thought.'

'What?'

'You married the right man.'

I'm completely mystified. 'How come?

'He was called Burden. And you've carried a heavy burden all these years. Oh, I don't mean to suggest *Lewis* was a burden, only that you've had an over-developed sense of responsibility and shouldered too many burdens.'

'Have I?'

'Yes. In a word. Now what you need is freedom – to be yourself. To enjoy life.'

'I like the sound of that.'

'Next time make sure it's a wise man.'

He departs with a wave, not waiting for my response.

I've returned to the dining room at Bradley Drive with renewed energy. He'll be back in nine days.

The upholstered chairs are assigned to the tip. No flame-retardant labels. Ironic, really. All this time Mother has been wandering in a twilight zone, playing with fire quite literally, and no one has torn these unsuitable possessions away from her.

While I'm already on my knees emptying the sideboard, I use the opportunity to peel back the carpet. It was laid in the era before gripper rods were invented and the tacks are in to stay. I can only manage to drag up one corner.

The newspaper lining the floorboards underneath is dated 1945. The end of the war. Before my memories begin. Perhaps when the room is empty and the carpet is rolled up for the tip, I'll have space to read some of it; to enter the world of my mother's hey-day.

I picture her spreading the pages, pausing to study a column that catches her eye. Dreaming perhaps of the children who would one day prance around on this same floor.

And it was in this very room that she surprised a burglar not long after they moved to Bradley Drive, a young lad, down on his luck. She sat him down in the kitchen, listened to his story, sent him away quietly with a full belly and a few pounds.

'You wouldn't do that today!' she said, wagging a finger. 'Nowadays they'd pull a knife rather than apologise. Things were different back then. Before benefits and allowances came in.'

'...*kind and unselfish*.' Aaron's words ring in my head.

Why couldn't life be more kind to her? It had stolen so much. Left behind an empty ruin.

As I stand up the decanter on the sideboard clinks against the glasses. My mind flips to a film: some Agatha Christie adaptation. Mother and I together watched the butler slip poison into the decanter before serving Lady Something-or-other at dinner. The decanter was washed out and refilled before anyone could suspect anything, never mind examine it. As I battled to get Mother to swallow her medication that night, the idea hustled into my mind – poison or medication, it can be the same thing. Just given in different quantities. How easy it would be to disguise the fact. Murder refashioned as a merciful act.

I shiver now, remembering. How vulnerable she was... how close I came. But for the grace of God...

The massive table with its extra leaves will accompany the sideboard. It'll be a wrench to see it go.

How many family milestones it has witnessed. Birthdays, Christmases, funerals, reunions. I suddenly want to hold one more special occasion, on this very table, in this room... to bring Mother back to her rightful place, presiding over the family she created.

I crumple onto the chair she occupied for so many years. The force of her incapacity hits me. Very soon all that will remain will be the 'whine of dementia and the hieroglyph that looks like her'. I read that in a book I was glancing through yesterday. It made the hairs on the back of my neck stand on end.

By the time James arrives, I have stripped two walls of paper.

'Dare I enter?' he hisses around the door.

'Yes, the stepladder's over this side,' I call.

'I was thinking more of stepfathers than stepladders!' he says, sidling in with a grin.

'Shush, James.'

'I am agog to meet this man who can make my mother blush.'

'I think Gran has done all we need to put him off, without you sticking your oar in.'

'So what did she do?'

'Oh, only treated him to a comprehensive display of all her worst tricks.'

'Oh dear. How did he react?'

'As if he saw this kind of thing every day and I was making a mountain out of a molehill.'

'Well, you do take Gran's behaviours too personally, you know.'

I stare at him for a long moment. 'Do I? Aaron said something like that.'

'Well, you do, sometimes. It's the Alzheimer's making her do these things. She can't help it. You can't help it.'

'But she's my mum.'

'So? Am I responsible for what *you* do? Heaven forbid!'

In spite of myself I feel the clouds lift.

'Mother, you have to stop worrying and accept that this bloke is as keen as mustard. He doesn't care what your crazy family is up to. He sees you – hard-working, loyal, warm-hearted, little old you. And it's you he wants.'

James' banter keeps me from dwelling on the doubts. But when I collapse into bed at midnight, sleep evades me in spite of the physical exhaustion.

I am not the woman James and Aaron think I am. I'm not. I've felt hatred for my own mother. I've shaken her. I've tried to drown her. I've walked away and tried to pretend she doesn't exist. The fact that I've stepped back from the brink is more a measure of my cowardice than anything else. The return of warmth and tenderness now is thanks to the dedication of the carers at The Morningside, relieving me of responsibility, not to my forgiving nature.

This tendency to put family carers on a pedestal, to laud their self-sacrifice, merely adds to my burden. I gave up. I couldn't do it. I put my mother into a home. Adeline and Aunt Beatrice were right: her place is in the family. I should have listened to them. I don't deserve happiness built on my rejection of her. Nor do I merit praise.

Forgive me, Mum. Forgive me. Tomorrow I'll come to see you. Tell you I'm sorry. Sorry I failed you.

Maybe I *will* arrange one more party at your table.

Chapter 8

AARON RINGS ME every evening on my landline, 'To make sure you go home and get your beauty sleep.' And I know I need that! I've become so much more conscious of wrinkles and aches, of late.

Ours is a strange courtship. Dusty clothes, hard work, the smell of paint and plaster, have given our relationship the ease of a long cohabitation rather than the thrill of a new romance. We are too tired to pretend. But as we work we talk.

He tells me about Gisela: her artistic temperament and skills, her bouts of depression, her long struggle with emphysema. Their marriage – 32 years – more stormy than Aaron would have liked.

A softness enters his voice as he speaks of his two daughters. Jacquiline (a French spelling at Gisela's insistence), born with a hare-lip and cleft palette; an opportunity for her father to feed her with specially designed cups until the cleft had been repaired and healed. The bond they still share. Jesslyn, the tomboy in the family, the rebel. He worries about her impulsive behaviour. He shares photos of his adored grandchildren; three already, a fourth on the way.

It's easier to trade my own experiences of life in exchange for his. Marriage, siblings, teaching. Husband, children, grandchildren. Weaknesses, intolerances, hopes. No secrets.

I'm ready to introduce him to James.

But it's Pandora he speaks to first.

We're sorting out papers in the den, the room my father called 'his' before two sons steamrollered through the whole notion of privacy. It's odd, now I pause to think about it, I feel no compunction about allowing Aaron to read these family documents. Aside from James I can't think of anyone else I would allow to be involved in this task, but I'd gladly hand the whole thing over to him. His legal brain will separate the wheat from the chaff far better than I can.

The sheer size of the job, never mind its complexity, is formidable. After Father's death my mother retrieved the essential papers to take care of the funeral and his will, and then closed the door on this room. It remained unused. But once the fog descended, it became all too common to discover her in here, emptying drawers, pulling files, flicking through books, looking for who knows what? Harassed beyond reason, I'd bundle everything away to create an illusion of order, but I'm embarrassed now by my slovenly practices.

I'm in the middle of arranging certificates of completion from building control in chronological order, when the phone rings in the hall. Aaron answers it.

'Hello, Pandora.'... 'A friend of your mother's. Aaron Wiseman.'... 'Yes, of course. I'll go and get her for you. One moment, please.'

By this time I'm at his side. He smiles and gives me a swift hug before passing me the receiver.

'Pandora. Sorry. I was sorting Gran's papers.'

'Who's *that*?'

'A friend of mine. A solicitor. He's helping me with clearing Gran's house.' And so much more. But that can wait.

'Well, I was wondering if you could have Max on Friday for the weekend, please. Something's come up and I need to go away. Karah's fine. She's happy to stay with a friend. But I'd be happier knowing that Max was with somebody who'll watch him properly.'

'Yes, of course I'll have him. I'd love to.'

'Thanks. If I bring him over at five, is that OK with you?'

'Five on Friday. Yes. I'll make sure I'm home by then. And it'll be nice to have a weekend simply being a grandmother.'

Aaron pulls a face when I tell him about Pandora's request. His own plans for me must be put on hold. But I'm definitely not ready for Pandora's reaction to his place in my life.

He shrugs. 'Well, my own grandchildren will no doubt use the bonus time to quiz me about my absences from home. My daughters are too suspicious to ask outright!'

To compensate, Aaron suggests we give ourselves tomorrow off. 'Just to be together.' He's always wanted to see the Trossachs.

Aaron, Max, the house... the days slip by and my burden of guilt grows. I *must* visit Mother. What happened to my resolve to visit her daily?

She's wearing a yellow cardigan when I arrive. Yellow! It's tantamount to having someone else's false teeth in her mouth. Her own muted shades lie neatly in the drawer. Undisturbed. She no longer even rummages.

Her pale skin is almost translucent.

'Come on, let's go out and see the roses. Dad grew roses, didn't he? You always loved them.'

The scent from the borders envelops us. I keep up a trickle of conversation: '*Ena Harkness*, Dad's favourite... *Peace* – too wishy-washy, he always said... *Apricot Nectar* – heady perfume but raggy flower.'

She shuffles along for a few minutes, then starts pulling back.

'Oh, it's such a lovely day, let's stay outside.'

She takes no notice.

'Should I insist?' I ask the carer who's holding the door open for us.

'Difficult to insist if she won't go. Maybe try again later.'

We repeat the excursion three times. Same route. Same roses.

Same comments. Same attention span.

Back in her room she's just as restless, standing up, sitting down, wandering round her bed, back again, over and over and over again. She strips off the yellow cardigan and fumbles with a rose-pink one. She peels it off again. She gets up again leaving a spreading wet patch behind her.

While the carers clean her up I sit in the garden.

Aaron's words echo in my mind.

'*It's the Alzheimer's making her do these things. She can't help it. You can't help it.*'

But it *feels* deliberate.

Birgitte, one of the carers I've grown to know and like, finds me. 'All done. But you look exhausted.'

'Oh, you know. It's only Mother. And the house.'

'Why don't you take a break away from this place? Go somewhere nice. Pamper yourself for a while. Or let that nice man pamper you.'

I sigh. 'I know you're right. I'm not much use to Mother if I'm so tired I haven't got the patience with her.'

'I was meaning for your own sake. Doris will be OK. We're here to take care of her. But *you* need a break to stop yourself from cracking up. I've seen it before. You dedicated ones are all the same. Knock yourself into the ground before you'll concede that you have needs too.'

'I'll think about it.'

I know I need it. It was Aaron who brought me face to face with my own lack of sensitivity, the impatience that left Mother behind.

It was on his third visit to her that I saw it first.

'George? Are you George?' she asked him.

'No, Doris. I'm Aaron. But this is George. Look. George.' He picked up the photo of Dad from her bedside table. 'What a handsome man.' A pause. 'And I hear he was very good with his hands.' Pause. 'I've seen the tree house he made at Bradley Drive. I'd love to be able to create something as clever as that.'

He stopped talking and moved the picture closer. She was staring.

'George,' he said softly, watching her. 'This is George.'

For a long moment they sat side by side, both looking at the picture, as if sharing something precious. Then she started to move her hand towards it. He reciprocated. Her fingers hovered, touched the glass.

'George,' he whispered.

'George,' she repeated.

Once her attention wandered, he replaced the photo and talked to me, giving her space. And then...

'We have something in common, you know, Doris. You have a daughter, Jessica. Here she is, look. Jessica. Jess.'

'Aaron,' I remonstrated. He reached out to lay a hand over mine, but kept his eyes on Mother.

'I've got a daughter with a similar name. Jesslyn. We call her Jess sometimes. Jessica. Jesslyn. Two Jesses.'

My mother peered at him. 'Did I invite you?'

'No, but I chose to come and see you. And I'm very pleased to meet you.' She was so still I half-expected her to reach out to shake his hand. He waited a minute and then spoke again, this time in a different tone. 'I came with Jessica. Your daughter. Your lovely daughter, Jessica. Here she is. She visits you often. You're a very lucky woman to have a daughter like her.'

And somehow he managed to soothe her with his quiet words. Simple, positive words, that didn't challenge or threaten or cast doubt on her distortions.

As soon as we were outside, I asked him, 'How did you learn to do that?'

'After Gisela died, I decided I needed to do something useful. Volunteer somewhere. Help get things in perspective, stop me brooding. I started to visit our local residential home. Only an hour or two a week to start with. I had absolutely no idea how to manage some of the residents I met, so I enrolled on a course. It was designed for proper carers, but I learned some useful tips. Basically they taught that you have to enter into the mind of the person with dementia, try to understand their world and respond appropriately. The bits I remember are, don't ask questions and don't contradict them. And you look for things they still relate to. I'm not very expert at it, but sometimes it works.'

'You're better at it than I am!'

'Nonsense. I'm a mere novice compared to you. You've been keeping your mum going for years. I've seen her a few times – for short visits. And this is the first time I've said anything more than the common civilities to her. You'd soon see how superficial my skills are if you watched me for long enough. Beginner's luck, today. Nothing more. Or maybe your mum was so overwhelmed by a strange man appearing with her daughter that she had to be quiet to assimilate the possibilities!'

'Beginner's luck or not, you're exactly the kind of person I'd like to visit me if I was confused and disorientated.'

'Well, isn't that lucky, then?'

Only then did I realise what I'd said. The colour leapt to my cheeks.

He smiled that smile that does something indescribable to my insides, and took my hand in his for the rest of the walk to the car. Before we got in he stopped and looked at me.

'Pity your mum's room doesn't overlook the car park.'

'Is it? Why?'

'I could kiss you here and she'd spend the next hour or two puzzling as to whether or not she really saw what she thought she saw.'

'I take back my admiration of your abilities. It's all a charade.'

'Or an excuse!'

I'm still wondering what else I don't know about this man who has raced back into my life before I can properly count the cost.

As we drive another thought strikes me.

'Aaron, can I ask you a couple of things in your professional capacity?'

'By all means.'

'You've seen what she's like. Is it all right, d'you think, for the doctors to use her for teaching purposes? Or is that some kind of abuse of her vulnerability?'

'Hmm.' He pauses. 'If they couldn't use someone else who could give informed consent, if their motives are exemplary, if it's done respectfully and if you've given permission, I'd say it's OK. Same as with research, I guess.'

'And what about giving her medication? They asked me that too. If she refuses to take her drugs, is it acceptable for them to disguise them in her food?'

'And you said?'

'It was. If she needs the medicine for health reasons, or for her quality of life. And if there's no other kindly way of giving them.'

'I agree. In an ideal world, one wouldn't want to deceive, but it might be the kindest option available in these circumstances. No merit in inflicting an unnecessary degree of distress for the sake of a principle.'

'Is it right, me deciding?'

'A team approach is best, I'd say. A consensus decision – you and the medical team. You all look at what you know about her and her previous values and opinions. And you decide what's in her best interests. And you document everything – the process as well as the decision. Records are so important. Sorry, I sound horribly lawyerish.'

'Not at all. I can't tell you how comforting it is to have you to share all this with. It's like having my own personal helpline and legal advisor.'

'As far as I'm concerned, I'm here for as long as you want me.'

He reaches across to cover my hand with his.

It's the end of the month before the next enigma distracts my attention. And I don't know what to think.

It's James who drops the first bombshell.

'Mum, did Aaron tell you I've been consulting him about Gran's affairs?'

I stare at him in amazement. 'No.' I know they've met formally now. I set that up myself. But discussing things behind my back?

'I like him. And trust him. He's got a shrewd head on his shoulders and he's an experienced solicitor. I value his advice.'

'Well, I'm very glad you like him, but what kind of things d'you need him for?'

'Legalish things. Nothing for you to worry about. Honestly. You know I wouldn't do anything that wasn't in your best interests. Or Gran's. And neither would Aaron. He's nutty about you, you know, Mother dear.'

I refuse to be distracted. 'But we've got our own lawyers to sort things out.'

'Heck! You won't find anyone more your "own" than Aaron! Don't you trust him?'

'Of course I do!'

'Well, there you are then. I'm feeling my way with some of this and it helps to check things with him.'

'Is this about the papers and things he's been sorting in the den?'

'No. Mostly the stuff we drew up with Gran's lawyer and the finances.'

'Well, just remember, James – I don't want there to be any suggestion of favouritism for me, or for you. We agreed. It must all be perfectly fairly distributed. No preferential treatment.'

'Absolutely. And having another pair of eyes, another legal brain, somebody who doesn't stand to gain, helps in that process.' He grinned at me. 'Of course, the suspicious minds amongst us might be thinking Mr Wiseman *is* expecting to benefit at some future date from anything you inherit.'

I stare at him, appalled by the suggestion.

'I'm teasing you, Mum! Aaron has no intention of capitalising on your assets now or at any time in the future. It's you he wants, not your millions. Rest assured on that.'

'But would Adeline or Aunt Beatrice see it that way?'

'Do they know about this man in your life?'

'Certainly not! Nor incidentally does Pandora.'

'Ah. So when d'you intend to tell her?'

'I don't know. I think it'll just happen.'

'Would you like me to tell her?'

'No, dear. But thank you. I *will* tell her. But I don't think the time's right yet.' And I can't find the words to tell her. 'I think... Oh James, I'm so worried about her. I think things aren't right between her and Enrico. She hasn't said so, not in so many words. But reading between the lines...'

'And the last thing she needs is hearing her mum is in love and hearing wedding bells, eh?'

'James!'

'Well, if you aren't yet, I'm pretty sure he is!'

I know that's true, but it can wait. Pandora's needs come first. We mustn't do anything – *anything* – that might precipitate a rash decision. And as long as I don't 'interfere', maybe things will settle down.

That night, when we've packed away our tools and we're back at my house, sitting in the conservatory as the light fades from the garden, drinking hot chocolate, I find myself raising another troubling thought with Aaron.

'Can I talk to you about dementia? And my mum?'

'You can talk to me about anything you like. You know that.'

Lewis' struggle with conversation flashes into my mind. I force it back behind bars.

'When Mum was first admitted to the home, the doctors asked me what I wanted them to do if she collapsed or became ill and needed resuscitation. I knew she didn't want her life prolonged. She told me that. So we agreed, no heroics. But she's not the same person, now. Would she still say the same? What d'you think?'

'I'd say so. I think it would be more tricky if she was now a totally contented person in her own little world.'

'Well, she's certainly not that! She's a lost soul, but she's not what I would call a happy one.'

'So, in what way d'you think the decision might be different today?'

'Well, she's no longer aware of the state she's in, so that, in itself, doesn't trouble her. My fear is I'd be saying, "Let her go" because *I* don't want her to go on like this.'

Aaron watches me steadily, but this time it's not disconcerting, he's professional.

'You want my personal opinion on this?'

'Please.'

'Well, an advance directive takes account of exactly this kind of situation. Your mum's view was, "I don't want to have my life extended if that life is one of indignity and distress." She appointed you as her proxy, to represent her best interests once she became mentally unable to state her own opinion. And in my judgement, if that seems right from your perspective too, then that's a bonus and not something to be suspicious of.'

'And you're not saying that to make me feel better?'

He smiles. 'Now, much as it's my dearest wish to make you happy, I can think of far more satisfactory ways of doing so than spinning you a half-baked ethical argument. No, I'm telling you what I, in my best legal robes and wig, believe to be the case.'

'You are very good for my health.'

'Well, I'm pleased to know that at least!'

When I don't say more he asks, 'Is this all properly documented for your mum?'

'As far as I know, yes. I can't actually remember if I signed anything specific when she was admitted, but I think I did.'

'It would be worth checking. Maybe asking for an update to ensure what you want to happen does happen. And if you think I can help with wording or anything, then you have only to ask.'

'Thank you, Aaron. You've been brilliant through all of this. I don't know how I'd have managed without you.'

'Being the courageous woman you undoubtedly are, I'm sure you would have soldiered on, but it's been my privilege to be involved too.'

'You know, before you came back I often wondered what would have happened if you hadn't gone away. But I never imagined anything like this.'

'I was thinking that myself only yesterday, when we were painting. Would we have kept your mum with us and looked after her together? What would that have done to us? And if you'd put her in a home then, would you secretly have blamed me for forcing your hand? But this way... well, from where I sit, things look pretty much as good as they could get.'

'For me, too. But it could so easily have gone differently. I wanted Mum to get drugs to slow the disease down. I begged for them, from everyone I could contact. But nobody could, or would, get them. If I *had* managed to convince them, she might still have been with me when you came back.'

'So I'd have had to wait a bit longer.'

'I couldn't have asked you to do that.'

'And I know you wouldn't have. But I believe I would have done so,' he says softly.

For answer I get up and go to sit beside him, resting my head on his shoulder. His arm circles me and his lips move in my hair.

'I do love you.' It's the first time I've said it aloud. 'I don't deserve your patience but I'm so, so glad you *did* come back.'

He tightens his embrace.

'Before I respond to that in an appropriate manner there's something that's been nagging at me. When you sent me away last time, I went, I just wasn't sure how interested you were in me. And I could see that your mum was already beyond your care, but I felt I couldn't suggest you put her in a home, because it would have looked as if it was for *my* benefit. I've gone over it hundreds of times since, asking myself if I should have insisted you let me help. I'm still not sure, but if I was wrong to walk away, nobody regrets that more than me.'

He turns my face up to his and searches my eyes.

'It wasn't your fault,' I assure him. 'I was the one who sent you away. And it was only after you'd gone that I started to realise how much you meant to me. But I wouldn't have wanted you caught up in all of that mess. I'd have felt guilty about ruining your life too.'

His lips on mine chase any lingering doubt from my thoughts.

Much later he says, 'Sometime soon we must talk about the future – where, when, etc. That will keep until we've finished the house and provided for your mum. I know you can't think beyond that at the moment and I'm not going to press you. But there is one thing I need to check before it's too late. Would you want me to buy the Bradley Drive house?'

Something lurches in my stomach.

'Bradley Drive?'

'Mm. As in the house you grew up in. The house you plan to put on the market in September.'

'But I need the money for Mother....'

'I know you do. I'm not suggesting you *give* it to me. I could just bid higher than anyone else. That is, if you'd want to live there.'

It takes me an age to answer. 'Aaron, thank you... but no. There's too much baggage.'

'Fair enough. If you're sure.'

A thought strikes me. 'But perhaps we might keep the table, in case...'

'We can put anything you fancy keeping into storage meantime. Sensible thinking.'

We sit without speaking for a long moment. My thoughts are spiralling out of control.

Then an idea makes me smile. 'Imagine the reaction you'd get from Adeline or Aunt Beatrice if *you* bought the house!'

'Whoops! Indeed. Suspicions would definitely be aroused.'

'Oh, that would be nothing new. I'm already a money-grabbing, undutiful daughter in those quarters.'

'You can't win, can you, sweetheart? Your sister and aunt think you're bent on having a riotous life of your own, to hang with everyone else. James and I think you are way too conscientious and dutiful for your own good.'

I frown. 'Well, I do know my motives aren't mercenary but I wish you wouldn't exaggerate my selflessness. I mean it, Aaron. I feel I'm here under false pretences when you say things like that.'

'As in – here in my arms?'

'Yes.'

'Well, as to that, I can give you a thousand reasons why I still want you here in my arms whatever the level of your filial duty.'

But it's the following evening that the biggest shock turns my already chaotic world completely upside down.

It's late, but Aaron leaves in the morning, and I want to prolong every minute I can with him.

'James tells me he's been consulting you about Mum's papers.'

'Mm.'

'Thank you so much. You know how I hate all that business stuff.'

'You're welcome. It's no big deal.'

'It's terribly tempting to leave it all up to you two. But is there anything I *ought* to know about?'

He's silent so long I disengage myself from his embrace and look at him directly.

'Aaron? James said there were papers you found – the ones that he took to the solicitor. What were they about?'

'Well. I'm not quite sure how to answer the first question, but the second one helps to clarify things.'

'Meaning?'

'There *is* something. Only I wasn't sure if I should tell you.'

Something cold slithers into my veins.

'Is it the house? Is it money? Won't I be able to keep Mum

at The Morningside?'

'No, no. It's not money.' He stares at me for a long moment. 'Actually… it's confirmation of something I already knew.' He takes my hand in both his. 'Jess, darling, this is probably going to come as something of a shock.'

I stare at him. I don't like the feel of this.

'Remember when you asked about my mother admiring Doris? Saying how kind and unselfish she was?' I nod. 'And I said it was an old story. Long before our time.' It's hard to breathe. 'Well, it did have *something* to do with you. The thing my mum knew was that…' He tightens his grip on my fingers.

The pause goes on and on.

'Doris, she isn't actually your real mother, Jessica. She adopted you. And I found the documents in the den that confirm that.'

When I can unstaple my tongue I manage, '*Adopted?*'

He nods.

'But my birth certificate…'

'Seems to say you're Doris' daughter?'

'No. It doesn't *seem* to say that. It *does* say that!'

'I guess that fits with what my mother told me. Doris adopted you at birth. She had her name put on your birth certificate. And all before she had any children of her own.'

It can't be true. There must be some other explanation. But the documents…

'So, who's my *real* mother then?'

He shakes his head. 'Mum didn't say. I didn't ask. But does it matter? Now?'

'Yes. No. I don't know. I can't think straight.'

'I'm desperately sorry to drop this on you, sweetheart, on top of everything else.'

The ramifications are racing through my head.

'And my dad…?' The bottom drops out of my world. Not Dad. Not *Dad*. Please, don't let it be true.

He shakes his head. 'I don't know.'

'But he said… he *told* me… when one of the girls at school

said I wasn't a real Mannering, he said…'

'He said he was your father?'

'Well, not exactly.' What *did* he say? 'He said… I took after Mum's mother.' I feel sick. 'He lied.'

Aaron holds me close. I fight the tears.

'Why didn't they tell me? Why didn't *anybody* say? My uncles, Aunt Beatrice, they all must have known.'

'Not necessarily. It was wartime. Doris was married, living her own life. It's perfectly possible nobody else knew.'

A new thought strikes me. 'What about your mother? Did she know anything else?'

'If she did, she didn't tell me.'

'And the papers don't say?'

'No.'

I go round and round searching for answers. There are none. Who am I?

'Why didn't you tell me before?' I say eventually.

'Well, remember how you said your mum was always searching in the den? I think it was for those papers. She must have vaguely realised there was something important, somewhere – something she didn't want discovered. So when I found them, I thought, would she want you to know? No. After all, she'd kept this secret all these years. I had no right to ignore her wishes now that she was past instructing me.'

'But you told James.'

'No, James doesn't know. For the same reason. I simply sealed the papers in an envelope and asked him to hand them to Doris' solicitor. It's for you to decide if he should know. Or anyone else.'

'So why did you tell me now?'

'You asked outright what was in the papers. I couldn't lie to you. You wouldn't trust me again. And my first allegiance is to you, not your mother. I don't have the right to deny you knowledge that concerns you directly. Not when you specifically ask for it.'

'Thank you, Aaron. Thank you for being so *scrupulous*.'

'I hope it *was* the right thing to do.'

'It was.'

My whole body is trembling. He wraps me in his jacket and holds me close.

The grandfather clock strikes 2 a.m. before I remember Aaron has a long drive south in the morning.

I start to disengage myself but he tightens his hold.

'I so don't want to go. Especially right now.'

Chapter 9

PANDORA TELLS ME over the phone in a breathless rush.

'I've left Enrico. I should have done it years ago. But for the sake of the children... We've had a trial separation before, but this time it's for good. And yes, before you ask, it's because he's been unfaithful. Again! Some woman in Italy he's known from childhood. Well, she's welcome to him. I won't be taking him back. He says he won't contest the divorce.'

I want to drop everything and drive across to see her, but Pandora is adamant: she wants to forget it, move on.

'Things will be easier now it's out in the open and I'm officially a single parent. I get the house and the contents, he doesn't want them. He's going back to Italy, to live with this floozy. He's promised to provide for Karah and Max – he can afford it – so their lives won't be disrupted. I told him I won't have the children upset over this. I want them to go to the same school, have the same friends, carry on as normal. I'll be fine. Things could be a lot worse. To be honest, Mum, I'm glad it's over. We're better off without him.'

Behind the bravado she's suffering much more than the end of a marriage. Being rejected for another woman will damage her in ways she perhaps hasn't yet fathomed.

'Does James know?'

'No. I haven't told anyone. Tell him if you like. But I don't want either of you to come over, sympathising. I mean it, Mum. It's finished. This is a clean slate. The start of the rest of my life. I'm fine.'

Poor Pandora. Trapped in a cocoon of distorted values. Her own worst enemy.

So what if Doris is not my birth mother? So what if mystery monies have been coming into her account for years? So what if there's a persistent leak in the conservatory roof at Bradley Drive?

I've chosen 'Gentle Gold' for the walls out here in the conservatory. It's warmer than magnolia but I think still bland enough not to be intrusive. Mother would approve.

Mother... curious, when I'm not thinking about it, she's still just Mother. But knowing she's not, I have so many questions. Should I ask my uncles? Or Aunt Beatrice? Probably not. No point in disturbing them if they never knew. Should I tell James? I doubt it would make any difference – she's his pal anyway. And Pandora's got enough confusion in her life already.

Does knowing make any difference to *me*? It can't change anything that's gone before, that's for sure. I can't go back and reject responsibility. I can't reclaim my career, my freedom. But... should I be the one to hold her power of attorney? Should James? Or should someone else manage her affairs? Who could do it? Who would?

And what about her will? Maybe I'm *not* entitled to decide to sell the house. Is this why she stipulated it can't be seen until after her death?

Mother's always been a force to be reckoned with. Physically strong too. Five foot one and slim she might be, but she could wield an axe or dig a plot as effectively as any agricultural labourer. I can see her yet, out in all weathers, manhandling stones for the rockery, sawing off branches in the orchard, up to her thighs in the pond, clearing the blocked drain. Father was altogether gentler and less driven.

It was Mother's vision and hard graft that created the amazing garden of our childhood years, so it was a shock finding out that she'd sold the first tranche of land without consulting any of us. Five-storey flats replaced the orchard; a sprawl of garages covered part of the vegetable plot. The uninterrupted view to the Pentland Hills which we once took for granted as our birthright, was no more. But Mother's 'excuse' was, she needed ready money and she needed it now.

It all began with a letter. Her brother, Jack, writing from America: the doctors had given him three months at most. Long since separated from his wife, Betty, he was on his own. Mother flew out that week and nursed him through his final weeks.

Less than a year later, Eugene got married and settled in Australia. Mother instantly set about lessening the distance between us all. And in time a second swathe of the garden was bulldozed. Two bungalows stood where once we had scampered over the rockery and scavenged for tadpoles.

Mother refused to waver: 'Nobody owns this earth. We only borrow bits of it. And people are much more important than possessions.'

From the conservatory today I look out on what's left of the land Mother owns. James has been practical, paring things back to the essentials. Ready for a modern family. But he couldn't bring himself to take down the old apple tree.

'Our first swing hung from that. I remember Dad pushing me high enough to see into the kitchen window. Gran was making scones for our mid-morning snack. She wrapped them in fancy serviettes and popped them in little bags with funny faces on them, and we ate them down by the stream, still warm.'

'Happy days,' I sighed.

'They were, Mum. Gran was brilliant. Remember the time she took Pandora and me to York and we missed the train home? We had hours to wait and she invented such great games we were almost sorry to leave that magical platform!'

'And she was always telling you stories.'

'And she taught us to knit.'

'And remember the special wee plot in her garden for you children?'

'Which was always bursting with colour, as I recall.'

I laughed. 'I rather think she stuck flowers in when things were getting a bit dreary, to keep you enthusiastic.'

James grinned. 'Probably, knowing Gran. Maybe that's why Pandora can't tell a dahlia from a daisy! Pansies probably appeared where she'd planted poppies.'

We savoured the memories in silence.

Mum kept an album of photos taken in the garden over the decades. My favourite ones were of the summer Dad was 40. The garden was stunning that year and we held the party outside. And there was Mum, surrounded by her family and her flowers, undisputed queen.

Nowadays it's too painful to look at those shots. The contrast is too sad. There's the gate covered in her favourite rambling rose – she left it unlatched and Karah toddled out into the road. There's the holly tree we raided annually – scorched to death by the bonfire she made to burn the cot and the baby clothes; the twin junipers, background for so many close-ups – linked by her red scarf the night she wandered down the street leaving the gas on, unlit, and the front door wide open.

And now we're preparing to hand over what's left of this garden to strangers.

When Aaron rings I'm still at Bradley Drive.

'You sound weary, sweetheart.'

Just sharing the news about Pandora helps. He says all the right things.

'And how's the conservatory looking?'

'Lovely. Especially in the sunshine. James fixed the radiator last night, so I've only got to sweep up and wash the floor, and then get the tiles down.'

'Why don't you leave that for me? I'll be up again at the weekend.'

'Thanks, but I'm happy to do it. Stops me moping. That's

why I've stayed late. Besides, I'm hoping to be *finished* by the weekend.'

'You're amazing. And don't forget, once it's done – you agreed – you're coming away on holiday. No more excuses. Two whole weeks of having you all to myself, I can't wait.'

'Me too.'

'I won't hold you up right now, but I wanted to tell you how much I love you.'

I have all the time in the world for that.

I didn't expect James tonight. He arrives as I start the tiling.

'Up you get. I'll do that.'

'But...'

'No buts. You've done enough. I could murder a cup of tea, though.'

I leave him to the job and hoover through the finished rooms. The end result has exceeded my expectations. So why do I feel so low? That's what James wants to know when he finds me in tears in the sitting room.

'Mum? What's up?'

'Oh, nothing... I expect I'm just tired.'

'Well, that's nothing new. Come on. What's up?'

I hardly know myself.

'Aaron hasn't run off with a leggy blonde half his age, has he?'

I can't help but smile. 'If he has, he hasn't told me! No, it's not Aaron.'

'Pandora?' he prompts.

It's enough. He listens while I tell him about his sister, his aunt... and his grandmother. All the things (except one) that are preying on my mind, stopping me enjoying the triumph of the almost-completed house. He sympathises but is phlegmatic as usual.

'"God grant me the serenity to accept the things I cannot change; the courage to change the things I can; and the wisdom to know the difference." You're not going to change Pan, or

Aunty Adeline, or Aunt Beatrice. Nor Gran. But you've got to find the courage to get away on holiday, Mum. You're exhausted. That's why everything's getting on top of you.'

Before he leaves he turns and asks, 'I nearly forgot, how was Gran today?'

'Subdued. They've changed her medication. Again.'

'For?'

'What they call "challenging behaviours".'

James surprises me with a bellow of laughter. 'What a hoot! Trust Gran.'

'What's so funny about that?'

'Gran still challenging people. She was ever thus.'

'No. This isn't a nice kind of challenging. This is a what-on-earth-are-we-going-to-do-with-this-old-lady kind of challenge. She can be quite horrible at times, James. I hate to say it, but she can. Vicious even.'

'Needs an ASBO, does Gran!'

'It's not amusing, James. She's strong enough to hurt people, you know. She'd be appalled if she knew.'

'Ahah. You're back to the should-we-shouldn't-we thing, yes? That's what's upset you.'

'Well, wouldn't she be better off... dead.'

'Is her life so awful?'

'Who knows. We can't get inside her head.'

'If it was you, what would you want?'

'I'd have wanted to opt out right at the beginning.'

'Would you?' He's looking at me intently now.

'Definitely. And if it happens, that's precisely what I intend to do.'

'I hope you don't mean that.'

'Oh I do, James. There's no way I'm going to let you go through what I've had. Absolutely no way.'

'But I wouldn't want you to – opt out, I mean.'

'Not even to avoid all the humiliation, the distress?'

'For your sake, maybe, but not for my own. No, course not. You're my old mum. Ain't got no other. And I love you so!' he sings to disguise his emotion. I'm not fooled.

'And I love Gran too. I don't want to lose her either. But is this shell really still my mum?'

'Can they sort her out so she's placid and just pottering along, not hurting anybody or anything?'

'They don't know. That's what they're trying to do, only they don't want to turn her into a zombie.'

'But there again, the worth of your life doesn't depend on how you behave, does it?' He isn't expecting an answer. 'She's still my Gran. And I'd miss her.'

The silence spills out over the garden as the first duskiness of evening settles over the shrubs we've planted for the next incumbents.

'What does Aaron say?' he asks.

'He thinks we should respect her previous wishes, when she was competent to decide.'

'Spoken like a true lawyer!'

I reach across and pat James' hand. 'Thank you, love.'

'What for?'

'Accepting Aaron like you do.'

'He's exactly what you need.'

How true.

'Besides which, I like him.'

Chapter 10

I CAN'T PROCRASTINATE any longer. Pandora answers the phone on the seventh ring, just when I'm starting to think she's not in.

'Hello, love. How are you?' I say.

'Fine, we're all fine. How about you?'

'I've had a good day. Gran was better than she's been for ages. I think it's the new medication. I'm sure she remembered Grandpa's rose arches, and the lad from down the road stealing the flowers to sell in the market.'

'She said all that?'

'Well, no. Not exactly. I reminded her about it, and she smiled as if she still thought it was funny.' Thanks to Aaron. I owe him so much.

'Oh.'

'Well, I guess you had to be there.'

'You sound tired. So, when are you coming down, Mum?'

'Well, there's a slight complication.'

'Mum! You *promised*.'

'I know, dear. It's just that...'

'You can't leave Gran. I know. But, Mum, the way you're going *you*'ll be in a loony bin, and she'll still be pottering up and down those corridors, wetting herself and asking if she invited you!'

'She can't help it.'

'No, but *you* can! *We* need you too, you know. It was going to be a surprise, but I may as well tell you: Karah's got a big part in her drama group play. And Mrs Galsworthy's having a little concert – exclusively for parents and grandparents. Max'd be so chuffed to have *his* nana there to hear him play his guitar. Please come.'

'I will, dear, for a few days, but...'

'OK. That's settled. It's time somebody spoiled *you*.'

'Well, actually, Pandora, there's somebody else who's spoiling me now.'

'Who?'

'His name's Aaron.'

'That man? The one on the phone?'

'Yes.'

'You're *seeing* him?'

'Well, yes. And now... he's taking me on holiday.'

Long after she's put the phone down I'm staring blankly into space. I haven't the energy to move. 65? I feel 95.

'Listen to your own heart. You're important too. What you really want.' Aaron's wisdom seems to come to me so often these days.

And what does my heart say? No question. I want to be with him, to be a normal woman. To love someone who wants me for myself, not for what I can do for them. Who can still my conscience as far as Mother is concerned. And he's right. I do need a holiday. I've agreed to one.

'A measly 14 days, that's all. Far too short for me, but I'll settle for that for the time being.'

'But what if something happens when I'm not there?'

Aaron shakes his head at me. 'It's all documented. No heroics. You need a break *now*. Not *n* years from now.'

James has promised to pop in to see her while we're away. And like Pandora says, my mother *is* well cared for. The staff are kind and attentive. I've never seen any unkindness or impatience to speak of. How they do it is beyond me. Day in, day out. One patient nearly killed me.

But before we go there's one thing more to decide. What if Aaron wants an answer?

I thought I had it all buttoned up – 'before'. No one was going to listen to me going round in ever-decreasing circles... or haul me back from scaring some motorist half to death by wandering naked along an unlit road... or find I'd smeared smoked salmon and prawn medley all over their raspberry cheesecake... or know the urge to stuff my mouth with the resultant goo and tie a tablecloth very tightly over my nose and mouth... or to stick my head in the lavvy pan and pull the flush. Over and over again.

Oh yes, I've been there. But not James. Not Aaron.

So. My answer? Let's enjoy today but not commit to tomorrow.

But that was 'before'. Now I have no idea at all what time bombs lurk in my genes. So is there any reason not to say yes to Aaron if he asks while we're away? I don't want to be swayed by the holiday atmosphere. I need to decide when I'm as close as I can be to real life.

I'm not sure...

I must get on. These endless mental acrobatics are more exhausting than all the hard graft.

It's the last lap. The cupboard under the stairs. If I crack on, I'll have time to fit in a trip to the dump before it closes.

Judging by the smell, I'd say this door hasn't been opened in years. It's as well Pandora isn't here with her allergies.

Old brooms and dustpans, baked beans, rags, crystallised figs. Nothing of any moment until... an ornate box wedged in between two cereal packets. The case is crested, lined with satin. Ah. *That's* where they went.

'My grandmother's pearls,' Mother explained, when I was about 10. She bit one, to 'show they're *real*', and I shivered at the sound. I didn't want to touch them; I wanted sparkly jewels, the princess sort, not dreary old pearls that make faces sad.

I put them on one side. Are they worth the expense of valuation? Aaron will know.

Behind all the detritus there's a neat stack of boxes; the work of a methodical mind. The first one weighs a ton.

Grandmamma's treadle machine! It always stood in her hall, with its tapestry cloth, an aspidistra, and a black pot full of buttons and coins and pins and bits of elastic. It belonged to her mother before her... it's at least a hundred and thirty years old. And I know it made the wartime wedding dress in those two black and white photos – 'the only ones we had taken'.

'Look at those terrible seams. Makes me cringe now,' Mother said. 'The tension had gone on the machine, you see. Thick flannel, parachute silk, it was all the same.' She sighed. 'But Mamma had begged and borrowed to get that material. We sewed it together, by the light of a Tilley lamp, using an old dress as a pattern.'

'Did you mind, at the time?'

She shook her head. 'Folk make too much of weddings nowadays. All that money, all that fuss. For a few hours of show. There's more to marriage than a perfect dress. The kind of attitude my mamma had – that's what gets you through the hard times.'

I sigh, now, thinking of Pandora. A fabulous dress. An expensive leather album of photos... Yes, there's more.

'*Rainy day*' it says on the side of the next three boxes. Each one crammed full with curtains and sheets – Mother's insurance against another war.

I'm deep inside the bend under the stairs now, my knees complaining. But only four suitcases to go, and then I'm done.

The first one bears the initials J.J.G. embossed in gold on the battered brown leather. Who was J.J.G.? Would my mother have known before the holes in her brain grew too large to retain anything? Inside are piles of newspapers. The war recorded for posterity. James might be interested. I slap on a post-it.

The second case is sturdier, reinforced at each corner. It has a sliver of a label stuck on one side, all the identity torn away. I gingerly peel back several layers of paper.

My heart races.

Encrusted fabric, fine pleating... the feel of privilege and wealth. What place has this in my mother's life?

I drag the case out backwards into the hall. The light from the stair window glints on beads and spangles as I lift it out with infinite care. Antique black, a ballgown made for someone an inch or two shorter than me... breathtaking in its elegance and craftsmanship. I hold it against myself and smooth the voluminous folds, then hang it on the door and turn back to the case.

More layers of smooth paper, something very like a flannelette sheet, and underneath that the softest duck-egg blue jacket, black frogging accentuating the shape – full bust, tiny waist.

I slip it on and strut in front of the hall mirror.

'*Well, good afternoon, m'lady.*'

'*Good afternoon, Holmes. Is the master in?*'

'*He is indeed, m'lady. In the drawing room. Shall I serve afternoon tea?*'

'*If you please, Holmes.*'

Kid gloves... a reticule complete with silver pomander... riding boots... a buttonhook...

How did such opulence come to be in my mother's possession?

The penultimate case is completely empty. No marks. Nothing to distinguish it. Except its quality.

The last one is dark green leather with a faulty catch. I take it out into the conservatory where the light is brighter.

Photographs. Dozens of them. Higgledy-piggledy. Exquisite portraits alongside blurred snaps with heads lopped off. My adoptive family. I'm so lost in weaving my own histories, that I hear nothing until I feel a kiss on the back of my neck.

I spin round.

'Aaron! I didn't know you were coming.'

'Somebody needed to come to Edinburgh today to see a client. I elected myself. Can't think why!'

He holds out his arms and I melt into them.

'Hmm. I can see I must surprise you more often if this is the welcome I get.'

I'm still poring over the photos when James arrives. I hadn't expected him today either.

'Aren't they amazing, James? See this. Somebody's wedding picture. Donkey's years ago. But look at the photography.'

'Wow! Does it say who it is?'

'May and Bertie. Wedding day. 2 June 1869.' What does this say underneath it – I can hardly read it.'

'Mamma's parents.'

'That would be Gran's grandparents,' I chose my words carefully.

'Your great-grandparents. My great-*great*-grandparents. Now you're talking. And you haven't ever seen this photo before?'

'Never.'

'They look awfully posh, don't they? I thought Gran came from a very ordinary family.'

'Well, I do know her grandmother "married beneath her" – according to Gran's great-aunt Hester anyway. She always spoke like a lady of the manor, apparently. People thought she was a bit uppity.'

'From this I'd say she had something to be uppity about! Maybe you've got a spot of blue blood in your veins, Mother.'

'You should be so lucky!' How can I disabuse him?

I turn the photos idly. The breath catches in my throat. It's a sepia portrait of the embroidered ballgown.

May. That's all it says. *May*. Great-grandmamma in her youth.

She's stunning: elfin face, a pile of dark curls threaded with ropes of beads, perfect figure. James is staring at her over my shoulder. He whistles appreciatively.

'How come we didn't inherit *her* looks? Eat your heart out, Pandora Montisoree.'

I trace the outline of her face with the edge of my finger.

'We've got this dress. It was in the cupboard under the stairs.'

'No kidding!'

I take him out into the hall and at that moment Aaron lets himself back into the house, complete with food from the supermarket. Somewhere I register that they seem unsurprised at the meeting.

'These must be worth a pound or two,' James breathes.

'They're priceless to me.'

He gives me a sharp look.

'Presumably May couldn't bear to part with such a fabulous outfit,' I say, touching the fanned sleeve. 'I wonder if she ever took these clothes out, tried them on. Regretted her decision.'

'Well, we'll never know now,' James retorts. 'But I'll regret it if I don't get my skates on and get home before Margot gives my dinner to the dog! We've got a parents' evening tonight, which I absolutely can't miss. I'll clear these boxes and then I'll be off.'

Between them they have the hall empty of boxes in record time.

'Not the black case, James. Please. I'll pack the clothes back in that. It's not heavy. I'll take it when I go. And the photos.'

His look is sharp again.

'Come home with me, Mum – both of you. You're exhausted. You've already put in a long day. Have a bite to eat with us.'

'Thanks, dear, but no. I need a little while longer.' I'm annoyed at the break in my voice and turn away quickly.

Aaron slips his arm around me – the first time in James' presence. 'I'll take good care of her, James,' he says quietly. 'Promise.'

'I know you will.'

'And we're almost there now.'

I lean into him, watching the car drive off, but then instantly turn back to the hall. The dress moves slightly in the draught. I see her...

No, I never knew you, May, but I'm not ready to say goodbye. Not yet.

'Jessica.' I turn at the strange note in Aaron's voice. 'Why don't you try them on? For me.' A long pause. 'Please?'

The light is golden in the conservatory as I glide towards him in my borrowed finery. His expression makes me say the first thing that comes into my head. 'I feel like a nervous teenager on her first date.'

His gaze slides over me slowly, a look on his face I haven't seen before.

'And I feel... breathless...'

'Before m'lady May.'

He shakes his head, holding my gaze. 'No. You. Looking so fabulous.'

'Minus the painting clothes.'

'Ah, I see you're determined to quell my romantic inclinations.'

'Only because...' The tears come anyway. He wraps me gently to him.

'I'm sorry. I don't know what's got into me. I'm not the crying type.'

'You, honey, are too worn out for words. I haven't begun to say a fraction of the things I intend to say to you, but they'll keep. Mercifully life has taught me a little patience. Although, when you look at me like that...'

I give myself up to his kiss.

I pack the clothes carefully back into the case. Aaron gathers up the photos.

One last look into the cupboard and I know my task is nearly done. I'll paint it tomorrow. Magnolia.

Aaron sits down on the bottom stair. 'Take your time, Jess. There's no hurry.'

The doors all stand open and my eyes roam over the bright rooms. This shell will soon echo to strangers' voices. But the last, most telling ghosts go with me. I turn to smile into Aaron's eyes.

'Thank you for being here today.'

DORIS

Chapter 11

2009

THE BOARD SAYS SUMMER. 29 August. A sun, smiling. I smile. Yellow. I hate yellow.

'You OK, Doris?' a blue lady says as she stomps past.

Doris? Doris isn't here. But *I* know where she is. Hiding. Hiding under the shed in our garden. Hiding from Papa.

Shhoo, shoo. Geddouta here, you dratted mutt!

Papa hates next-door's cat. Papa hates all cats. Especially Doris. He's put wire netting in the gap under the shed; *I'll stop that pesky blighter fouling up my garden!*

I like cats. I must find her. 'Doris. Dooooris.'

'You all right, dearie?' says a blue lady. 'Lookin' fa somethin?'

Where is she? 'D-ooo-ris.'

'How about you come with me. The pet lady's here this morning. With Araminta. Remember Araminta? The lovely fluffy cat. Remember? It'll be your turn to hold her in a bit. You like cats, don't you?'

It's black. Silky. Fat.

Mrs Green Cardigan picks her up, puts her on my lap. 'There we go, Doris.' Warm. I feel her breathing. I stroke her. She purrs under my hand.

Shhhh. Very softly. *Don't let Papa in. Don't! Don't!*

'Get him out of here!' I whisper, so the cat isn't frightened.

115

Mrs Green Cardigan picks her up. 'Somebody else's turn.'

Cuddling the cat has made me feel sleepy.

The kitten's eyes are still closed. I can feel its bones, thin sticks, all bunched up as it sleeps. Its little heart... beat, beat, beat. I walk ever so slowly up the path, holding it close to my chest. Keeping it warm and safe.

'Doris! Where did you find that?'

'Down by the shed, Mamma. Just lying there.'

'If I find you've lied to me, my girl...' Mamma's bristling as she scurries down the garden.

There are seven of them. Eyes closed. Huddled together. All black with white markings.

'Well, it's lucky for you your father isn't at home! We'd better get these wee things somewhere safe or that'll be the end of them!'

'Can I keep them in my bedroom? Please? I'll take really good care of them. Please, Mamma.'

'Absolutely not! And not another word on the subject, young lady!'

I hug the one I found closer to me. The claws scratch my skin as if to say, 'I'm doing my best to hang on to you.'

'What the hell are you doing?' My father's face is like a squashed bruise.

I try to push the kitten inside my jumper but his hand darts out and grabs it by its scruff. It mewls, its paws scrabbling the air.

He drops it into the heap of pulsating black fur and glares at Mamma.

'Get her inside. Now!'

I mustn't let...

'No! No! Please, don't!'

'Help!' It's the one in the mauve cardigan. I reach across...

Mrs Lavender gets up. Off comes the cardigan. Off comes the skirt. The water hisses down her skinny legs. I always wanted skinny legs. She's paddling. She smiles. I smile.

She sits down in the paddling pool. Her chest is like... contours... maps... Mr Cunningham... room 4a... third period Friday morning. *Get out your atlases.* Latitude. Longitude. Ridges. Mountains.

'Oh Gertie. Not again!' A blue lady. 'And you, Doris, look at you! Your slippers are sodden. You didn't need to step in it, did you? Really!' She calls. 'Ann.' Then louder. 'Ann, come and give me a hand, will you?'

'What's the magic word?' I say.

Another blue lady. 'Oh yuck!'

Ouch! It's Mrs Nippy Fingers.

'You're hurting me.'

'Get Doris outta here, will you, while I see to Gertie? Bung her slippers in the machine. She keeps shoutin' somethin' but I haven't a clue what she's sayin'. P'raps you can make it out. Any rate, get her away from this mess.'

Mrs Nippy Fingers scuffs her shoe. Her hands bite into my arm each scuff.

'Get off. Leave me alone! Mamma!'

'Whissht now, Doris. Let's get you out of these smelly slippers.'

The carpet's cold.

'Here, let me help you get Gertie up. Stand there, Doris. No running off, now. Come on, Gertie. Up you come, sweetheart. That's it. Look at you. What would your son say if he could see you in this state, eh?'

The knickers hang down like... like... like... that thing. Heavy. Veins. Batted from side to side when they walk.

I sit down. Close my eyes.

Uncle Frank's fingers stroke the udders, clip the machines on.

'Great bags of liquid nectar,' he says. 'Bigger the better, s'far as I'm concerned.'

The whole shed hums. Uncle Frank walks down the row, patting their swollen bellies, stroking their udders.

'There you are, old girl. That's good, in'it? Sweet. OK, *Doris.*
You're next.'

Their hooves skitter on the hard yard as they jostle to get
out, udders soft now against their scrambling legs.

You can't see the milk. But it's in there.

…

It's collecting. Pressing. Sore. Bursting.

The baby's fighting. Screaming. Biting down.

The pain!

'Engorged,' the nurse says. 'It'll get better once he's latched
on.'

He's screaming. Screaming.

'Bottle feed it, hen. Save yersel' the hassle.'

The pain! Take it away. I can't do it.

'Take it away! Take it away!'

'Doris? Hush, dear. Look who's here? It's your daughter. It's
Jessica.'

The old lady smiles. She's pretty. Nice eyes, but sad. Nice
smile. Lovely hair like… wavy hair… I can't remember.

'Hello, Mum,' Sad Eyes says.

Poor thing. A lost soul. Looking for her mother. Sad. I'll
invite her in. 'Cup of tea?'

'It's me, Jessica.'

Jessica?

'Why don't you take Doris out into the garden?' the blue
lady says. 'She'll need something on her feet, though. I'm afraid
we've had to pop her slippers in the wash.'

'Mamma?'

'I'm Jessica.' Sad Eyes leans close. Grey eyes. Tiny red veins.
Like… 'Let's go out and see the roses. You like roses.'

'You've got to get me out of here!' I hiss. 'They're going to
kidnap me.' It's so hot.

'Let go of my arm, Mum. You're pinching me.'

Maybe she didn't hear.

'They're going to kidnap me.' Right in her face this time.

'Ssh. There, that's better. Look at these roses. Aren't they lovely?'

Mmm. Lovely. Like a cloud.

'Oh, here's your favourite. *Ena Harkness*. Dad grew it for you. Mmm. Smell that.'

Her hand feels sticky... like Uncle Frank... 'Let me go!'

'Don't fight, Mum. Please. Just walk along nicely. That's better. This one's *Peace*. Dad always said it was too wishy-washy for him. Neither one thing nor the other. Remember?'

She pulls me along. She keeps bending down.

'Walk tall,' I say.

'*Iceberg... Queen Elizabeth... Blue Moon*.'

Once in a blue moon.

'*Buff Beauty... Cornelia... Céleste*.'

Céleste Murray. Ginger hair. In my class.

'Oh look. *Albertine*. Remember the arches we had, covered in *Albertine* roses? Fabulous perfume in the summer. Smell them.'

Mmmmmmm.

'*Versicolour. Rambling Rector*.'

Not in my church, thank you very much.

'*Himalayan Musk... Ingrid Bergman... Sweet Dream*.'

They all say that. The blue ladies. 'Sweet dreams.'

'Oh, look at that colour! You always liked the dark ones. Remember? What's this one? *Tuscany Superb*. Never heard of that before. Isn't that gorgeous?'

She's tugging me. Like Uncle Frank...

'No... no... let me go!'

I must get home before... If I run...

'No joy?' It's Fat Lady. 'But even a short time outside beats sitting in her room, I guess.'

This is my chance. I lean closer, hiss the words so they won't hear. 'You have to get me out of here. They're coming to get me.'

'You're OK, Doris,' Fat Lady says. 'You're quite safe. We'll look after you.' I can tell she isn't listening. She pats my arm but she's not looking at me; she's looking at Sad Eyes. 'The garden's fantastic this year, isn't it?'

'Fabulous! I only wish my roses grew like yours.' Sad Eyes smiles. She's pretty when she smiles. I smile.

'It's Tom. Best gardener we've ever had, I reckon.'

'My father grew roses. Mum always loved them. Should I have insisted she stayed out longer?'

Fat Lady shrugs. 'Who knows? You tried. It's all any of us can do.'

Another blue lady. 'Hi there, Doris. Hi, Jessica. D'you know she's bleeding, Ginny?' Mrs Tobacco-breath grabs my hand. 'Ach. You must have caught it on a thorn.'

'Oh, I'm so sorry.' Sad Eyes looks as if she might cry.

'No problem. We'll soon have this sorted, won't we, Doris?'

It stings. The blue lady sticks something on my hand. Is it poisonous? Is it radioactive?

'There we go. All better. Now you *look* at the roses, pet. No touching in future, all right?'

Roses? I want to see the roses.

Sad Eyes pulls my arm. She feels sticky... like Uncle Frank...

'I know you want to go on your own, but I'm just going to walk with you. It's for your own sake. There... look... your most favourite. *Ena Harkness*. Remember? Dad grew it for you. Smell that! And *Albertine*. Mmm. I can see those arches as if it was yesterday. Covered in blossom. D'you remember when Fergus Davenport sneaked in and cut all the low ones off and tried to sell them in the market? I always wondered what Dad actually said to him. All he said to me was, "Let's just say it's the last rose that little bugger will ever steal in all his long-legged life!" Poor old Fergus!'

Sad Eyes is laughing. Pretty. I smile.

'Oh, *do* you remember, Mum? You look as if you do!'

I look at Sad Eyes. 'Hannah?'

'No, Mum. I'm Jessica. Your daughter. Hannah was your mother. Remember? Your mamma.'

Mamma. Where is she? 'Mamma?'

'Mamma's gone now.'

Gone? Where's she gone? I must find her.

'No, Mum, you can't go in there. The door's locked. Let's sit down here and enjoy the sunshine and the scent. Have a wee snooze, maybe.'

The sun's warm...

Jack and Sydney are running. I can't keep up.

'Wait for me! Wait for me!'

'Come on, Doris! You've godda speed up if you wanna play boys' games.'

I'm going as fast as my legs will carry me.

Reuben comes up behind me, panting. He's not as skinny as the younger boys.

'Come on, kiddo. Hang on to me. We'll catch up.'

We fly over the grass, hand in hand. By the time we arrive at our new adventure course we're out of puff. All four of us flop on the ground and wait till our hearts stop pounding.

I'm up first. I'll show them. Girls aren't sissies.

I twist my legs twice round the rope. Since Reuben tied the big knot at the bottom, you get better purchase. Seven swings and I can see the roof of the factory.

'Hold on tight, Doris, you hear me?' Reuben's face comes and goes.

'I hear you.'

A few more swings and I'll touch the clouds.

They're cheering, Jack and Sydney.

'Higher! Higher!' they urge. 'Atta girl. Higher!'

I give it everything.

I only hear the first creak of the branch.

...

Somebody's wailing. 'She's dead! I know she's dead! We've killed her.'

Next thing I know their faces are all upside down. Somebody's shoving something sharp right up my back.

    'Doris! Doris! Wake up. Come on. Wake up!'

    'Mamma'll kill us!'

    'Don't move her. What if she's…?'

    Jack's slapping my hand. I bat him away.

    'Get off of me, you crazy loon. Get off.'

'Get off! Get off me!'

    'It's ok, Mum. You're fine. You were only snoozing.'

    'Reuben?'

    'Reuben's not here. It's just me. Jessica.'

    Not here? Where's he gone? I must find him.

Chapter 12

A year earlier

WHO'S MOVED IT? Who stole it? I need to find it...

'Help!'

'It's only me, Jessica.'

'Help! They're kidnapping me!'

'Mum! *Mum!* Look at me. What is it? What's wrong?'

Wandering in here, dragging me off. Wait till my father gets home. He'll sort it out.

'Papa! Help! Help!'

'Having trouble, Jessica?' It's Mrs Big Feet. 'Doris playing up today?'

'She seems really agitated about something.'

Mrs Big Feet marches in. One, two. One, two. Quick march. She pushes the button. They've gone.

'There. All gone, Doris.'

Gone? Who stole it?

'Sometimes they get frightened by the folk they see on the telly. You know? Not bein' able to make sense of 'em. Is that better, Doris?' Mrs Big Feet is in my face. 'Good show. OK, now all those other people, they've gone. It's just your daughter here with her nice gentleman friend, so how about you sit down here like a good girl and I'll bring you all a nice pot of tea and you can have a wee blether?'

Sad Eyes crouches. Too close. Don't touch me. Don't...

'Mum, d'you remember Aaron? He's come to see you again.'

'Hello, Doris.' Nice voice. Nice smile. Kind eyes.

'George?'

'No, I'm Aaron. But this is George. Look. George.'

George. Looking at me. Through the window. 'George.'

'That's right. George. Your husband. He's a handsome man, your George.'

George. George. George.

That Man is still sitting beside me. With George. Not touching. He knows. No touching.

'Did I invite you?'

'No, but I chose to come and see you.'

Kind eyes. Crinkly. Smiling. I smile.

'That's nice. You look very pretty when you smile. But I expect all the boys tell you that.'

I can see his teeth. White teeth. Not like...

'Knock, knock. Only me.' Mrs Big Feet. 'Here we go. A nice cuppa tea. And special pink wafer biscuits today, Doris. Mind and share nicely, now.'

'Thanks, Stacey,' Sad Eyes says.

She pours the tea. My job. That Man watches her.

'There you go, Mum.'

I taste it. Perfect.

'Looks good.' He's still here.

'Did I invite you?'

'You're very good about inviting people. A great hostess, I hear. I expect *you* make an excellent cup of tea as well,' he says, smiling.

I smile.

He takes the cup. 'Thank you, darling.'

Sad Eyes frowns. She's pink.

'You know, Doris,' he says, 'you and I have connections way back. So I'm trading on a long acquaintance in coming along to have tea with you.' He leans forward, speaks slowly. 'My mother went to school with your sister Beatrice.'

'Beatrice?' I ask.

'Yes, Beatrice.'

Beatrice. Beatr... Shsh.

'*Do* you remember, Mum?' Sad Eyes is crouching down again. 'Your sister, Beatrice?'

'Beatrice,' I say. I reach out and touch her hair. Soft **waves**. Pretty. Lovely eyes.

'That's right,' That Man says. 'My mother was Cecilia **Clar-**endon. Known as Cissy. Cissy?'

'Shsh.'

He leans closer to whisper. 'Sorry, I didn't know I **was** speaking too loudly,'

'Beatrice.'

'She said it again!' Sad Eyes says. 'I think she *does* remember.'

'Cissy told me some very nice things about you. She said you were one of the nicest, kindest girls she'd ever known.'

They're both grinning. I know they're plotting.

'But your daughter takes after you.'

'Beatrice.'

'That's right. She's your sister.'

'It's gone. Where is it? Gone.' I have to find it... Let me out of here!

'Sh, Mum. It's all right.'

She reaches into her bag. She's got it! She mustn't...

'Mum! *Mum!* Oh, look what you've done. Did you slop any of it on yourself? Are you hurt?'

'She's all right, Jessica. I think it was my fault. Let's talk about something different and give her space. I'd love another cup of tea, if there's any left.'

He hands me a duster. 'How about you get ready for the party? You do the dusting. Jessica will do the tea.'

Good. We'll be ready on time.

She gives him the tea. 'Why does she do that?' she says. 'You think she's fine and then, woof, off she goes!'

'They say that memories, feelings, are triggered that were upsetting in the past but the person can't access a mechanism for dealing with them. And that's scary. So you're supposed to find a cue that puts them back in a safe place – in this case cleaning the house in preparation for visitors – and they forget the troubling emotion. Or something like that.'

'So what happened there?'

'I have no idea. It was probably something I said. Or did. Maybe because I held her arm to steady the cup when she started to get up. Something simple like that. Or maybe because we were talking about Beatrice, she suddenly needed to find her... tell her something... make sure she was safe. Whatever. Anything can hold very different connotations for her. I don't know. It would take somebody much more experienced than me to sort it out. But I do know it's not her fault.'

Is she going to cry? He reaches out and touches her. Softly.

'Did I invite you?'

Nobody answers.

'I'm sorry, Aaron.'

'Don't be. I know it's much harder for you. How about we take your mum out for a run in the car? It might break the cycle of what's bothering her today. Shall we see if that's allowed?'

Sad Eyes is dragging me along with her.

'These pictures are nice, aren't they, Mum? See, this photograph. It's the Lake of Menteith. Beautiful, isn't it? D'you remember when we went there? For your 70th birthday? Seventy. Doesn't seem possible.' She looks at me. Grey eyes. Sad eyes. 'Little did we know then...'

He's coming. Closer. Closer.

'Hi, Doris. Morning, Jessica.'

'Good morning, Dr Griffiths.' Different voice. Who is she now?

'I was wondering if I might have a word? Perhaps in my office? Doris can sit on the balcony in the sun.'

'Has she been misbehaving again?'

'We'll talk about it in a minute, huh?'

Who's this coming?

'Oh, hi Frank. You just coming on shift?'

Frank! Get away! Don't touch me!
'Get away! Get away!'
Udders swinging. To and fro, to and fro. Veins bulging. Nipples dangling. Hands stroking. Smiling. Milk spurting. Your turn.

'No!'

'Steady, Doris. Steady now. Steady.'

The doctor's holding me.

'Let me go!'

Frank backs away. He shrugs. He knows.

He's going.

'Doris, I'd like you to make yourself comfy here on the balcony. Enjoy the sun, and the roses. Look, there's Tom weeding again. Jessica and I won't be far away.'

I close my eyes. I can only just hear them. They're plotting.

'So, how d'you think she is at the moment, Jessica?'

'I can't make out much of what she says now. Sometimes I think she remembers little things. She maybe smiles or looks sad in the right places. But... I don't know.'

'Right. Have you noticed anything else?'

'Well, she gets quite agitated sometimes – like just then. But it must be so awful for her not being able to make herself understood. Is it the frustration or the drugs... or...'

'Difficult to say exactly what's triggering it, but we're adjusting her medication gradually, till we find a level that keeps her calm.'

'And the violence, hitting out, is that all part of this?'

'It's all part of the dementia, yes. But hopefully this latest fine-tuning will help to calm things. We don't want to give her too much and make her like a zombie.'

'A friend was telling me about some technique, not drugs, where you find out what makes them feel safe and steer them in that direction when they start to get upset.'

'Ah yes. It's called SPECAL. We know about that. One of our senior nurses is going on a course to find out more about it and if it looks promising we could certainly try that with Doris. But until then we do need to manage your mother. Safely.'

'I'm sorry – does she hurt people? I mean, I can understand if she pushes *me* around. But I feel bad…'

'There's nothing for you to apologise for. You can't help it. Your mum can't help it. So please don't blame yourself. I'm only bringing you up to date with how we're playing things at the moment.'

'Thank you. I appreciate that. Is it anti-psychotic drugs you're giving her? I know you know more about it than I do, only I read that they can have adverse…'

The soil is warm. It's dark and damp where I've made the hole.

'A few inches deeper, Doris,' Mamma says. 'So the roots can spread out. If you loosen them like this, see how they all unravel. The pot stops them growing straight so they curl around and around. But now when you put the plant in the soil, the roots are all free and happy and they'll burrow down and down and down and find lots of food and water to make the plant big and strong.'

'Will they keep on growing and growing?'

'Yes.'

'Right down to Australia?'

'No, dear.' Mamma laughs. 'But keep digging. You never know what you might find.'

What I find is a matchbox. Funny. A matchbox in the soil. It's all damp and soggy. Inside is a skeleton.

'Mamma,' I whisper. It's like in church.

'Ahh.' She lets it out like a sigh. 'That was Joey. Your first goldfish. I don't expect you remember his funeral.'

I shake my head.

'Let's bury him again and then he'll help your new plants to grow, shall we?'

This time I feel the weight of the soil crushing Joey's bones as I shovel it back.

…

Lionel can't breathe. All that earth… 'No! No! No! Stop!'

'It's all right, Mum. You're quite safe. You were only dreaming. Just go back to sleep.'

That's nice. Her hand, stroking, gentle. Thank you, Mamma.

The floorboards squeak. 'Sorry about that.'

My eyes are heavy.

'How are you coping yourself, Jessica?'

'I still worry – did I do the right thing putting her in here, instead of keeping her with me.'

'That's a common experience for relatives. But think about it. It takes a full team of staff with lots of training behind them, 24 hours a day, seven days a week, 365 days a year, to meet the needs of these patients. You've had no training, and on top of the demanding physical work, you've had all the emotional strain, the heartache of watching your mum turn into a very different person from the woman you've known and loved all your life.'

'She's still my mother.'

'And you know her better than any of us. That's really why I wanted to have this chat. We've tried to encourage the interests and connections you mentioned, but is there anything else you can think of that might improve her quality of life, or help to calm her, or maybe stir a latent memory?'

I can't hear what she says. She's mumbling. I need to know.

He's crouching down. On one knee. Will you marry me?

She's snivelling.

'I'm sorry if I've upset you. You're exhausted, I can see that. D'you think you could give yourself permission to come in less often? Could you take a little time out for yourself without feeling like a traitor?'

More mumbling.

'You're the most important person in her life, but you won't be much use if you kill yourself in the process, will you?'

Killing? Who's killing? See! I knew it. They're trying to... the poor little kittens...

'It's not out of duty. I *want* to be here; I *want* to spend time with her.'

He's standing up. Sitting down. Not killing.

'I know you do. And we greatly admire your devotion, believe me. It doesn't happen in all families.'

'Would it have made a difference? If she'd had the drugs earlier, I mean?'

'Well, in fairness the most successful cases are where the drugs are combined with support – memory clinics, things like that. And yes, the whole package might have given you a few more months. But these drugs aren't ever a cure, it's important to understand that. Nobody ever claimed they were.'

'They wouldn't give us the other drug, either, the one for later on.'

'Ebixa. Yes, I'm afraid at that time the official recommendation was that Ebixa for advanced dementia shouldn't be prescribed on the NHS. We do use it here, and find it much better than the narcoleptics we used before. It keeps people calmer and sometimes helps them get more interest out of life.'

'I asked about those early ones for Mum, too. First of all they told me she wasn't bad enough, she'd have to get much worse before she qualified for that kind of treatment on the NHS.'

'Yes, indeed. And that too was received wisdom back then. The powers-that-be decided only to give what we call acetylcholinerase inhibitors — Aricept, Exelon, Reminyl — when patients had deteriorated sufficiently on the mini mental state memory test.'

'But then they said she was too far gone for them to be effective.' The voice has gone all quavery.

'I'm sorry.'

'It's not your fault. You've been very kind.'

'Well, thankfully, even in England and Wales the courts later ruled that doctors could exercise clinical judgement and give the drugs in certain cases. And up here, I might as well tell you, lots of us doctors working in dementia found creative ways of getting the drugs to the patients we felt would benefit.'

'I didn't know that.'

'And of course, your mum is getting all the medication she needs now.'

'But then I sometimes think, maybe it's the drugs that are making her do things out of character.'

'Damned if we do and damned if we don't, eh?' There's laughter running in and out.

Sad Eyes sighs. She doesn't laugh.

'D'you think she still knows me, somewhere inside?'

'I suspect on some level she's conscious of a familiarity, although whether she knows you're her daughter, or what that means is questionable at this stage. But *you* know she's your mother even if *she* doesn't. All I'm saying is, try not to exhaust yourself.'

Mmm. Quiet. *Peace...* wishy-washy...

The voices fade in and out. Somebody's playing with the machine again. Volume up, volume down. Up, down.

'...she's not aware...'

'...because she can't give her own informed consent...'

'...it seems wrong to make that decision for her when...'

'...in an emergency...'

'Oh, I don't...'

'...maybe death isn't...'

Reuben? Our Reuben?

'*I'm afraid so.*'

Not our Reuben.

'*The police came. Don't cry, Doris. It doesn't help anything. Be brave. Come on. Chin up.' My father's chin is up. Showing Mamma. Showing me. That's how it's done.*

He can't have. He wouldn't. Not our Reuben.

'*It stops us wondering,' Papa says.*

'*I always prayed,' Mamma says.*

'*Huh!' Papa snorts.*

Reuben. My big brother. He wouldn't *leave me. You don't understand.*

I have to find him. I know he's only hiding.

Mamma has tears running down her cheeks. Mamma? Crying? She never cries. 'We have to be brave, Doris. He's gone.'

It's dark. It's night-time. He knows I'm scared in the dark. He wouldn't. He just wouldn't.

'Reuben! Where are you?'

'Mum. Mum? Wake up. We need to move you. One of the other doctors needs to use this room.'

'Reuben?'

'Uncle Reuben's not here, Mum. He's dead. Oh, please don't cry. It was a long time ago.'

No! Not my Reuben. He can't be.

'Remind me again, who's Reuben?' That doctor's back. Go away. Don't look at me. I want Reuben.

'Her brother. Her oldest brother. She was very close to him. He died in his twenties. In South Africa. I shouldn't have said that. I forgot. But they told me, for her, it's like being told for the first time. '

No, no, no! He can't have died. Not my Reuben.

'Mum, we're going to go and find some lunch for you.'

'Lunch. Diddlysquat.'

'Did you hear that?' Sad Eyes is staring at me.

'What?'

'She said, "diddlysquat". It was one of her words. I don't give a diddlysquat. I wasn't worth a diddlysquat. And she just said it! I heard her! Oh Mum.'

I can hardly breathe she's holding me so tightly. Help. She's smothering me! Help! You've got to get me out of here.

She's smiling at me like...

It's catching. I smile.

Chapter 13
A year earlier

I'M NOT GOING in there. I hate the dark.

She's pulling me.

'Get off me. Help, somebody! Help. They're trying to kidnap me!'

'Can I 'elp you?' Foreign. 'Are you 'ere to see ze 'ome?'

'No. Actually, we're moving in today. If we can get inside the door, that is!'

She sniggers. 'I am Eva. Eva Bergovinska. One of ze carers. Pleased to meet you.'

'Jessica Burden. Good to meet you, too. And this is my mother, Doris Mannering.'

'Pleased to meet you, Doris.'

Doris indeed! I must get away.

'Hold on, Mum. Where are you going? No, this way. Let's go in with this lady.'

It's cool inside.

'Please to wait 'ere. I vill get somebody to show you to your mozzer's room.'

Mmmh. Nice smell. Good. Where's my duster? There it is...

'No, Mum. Leave it. Leave it. That's somebody's scarf. You've got one. See? Round your neck. See?'

Nice staircase.

Who's this?

'Hello!' She's very big. Black clothes. Black hair. Black face. Nice smile. Black and white smile. Liquorice Allsorts.

Warm hands.

'My name is Connie Norris. I'm the manager. But please, call me Connie.'

'Hello, Connie. I'm Jessica Burden.'

They're both smiling. I smile too.

'And you must be Mrs Doris Mannering. May I call you Doris? We like to be informal here. One big family.'

'Doris.'

'That's right. You're Doris. I'm Connie.'

The old one – I know her – she's smiling at me. Pretty smile. I know her from somewhere. 'Who are you?'

'I'm Jessica, Mum.'

'That's nice. Do I know you?'

'Yes, Mum. I'm your daughter.'

It's soft on the staircase. Quiet. I like quiet.

'And this is your room, Doris.'

'Isn't it lovely and bright and airy. And see, your own bathroom, all very handy. Only a few steps to go. Very nice. Look.'

'Excuse me.' A blue lady.

'Come in, Annie. This is Doris. We're showing her her new room. Doris, this is Annie. Another of our carers.'

'Hi, Doris. Sorry to interrupt, Connie, but Dr Maplethorpe's on the phone. Something about that blood result you wanted for Gertie?'

'Please excuse me, Jessica, I must take this call. But I'll be right back and then we'll go down and show you the lounge and dining room, Doris.'

'Oh, look at the view from the window, Mum! You can see right across to the Pentlands. Like we used to do from our house. Remember?'

Hills. I like hills.

'I specially asked for a room on this side. To remind you of home. D'you like it? Is it OK for you?'

'I want to go home.'

'Come and look at the garden.'

The room fills up. 'Here we are again. Remember me, Doris? I'm Connie. Now, shall we go and see the lounge and maybe some of the other ladies who live here?'

Sad Eyes is clutching my arm. She looks old when she stops smiling. She pulls me along.

She stops without warning. I bump into her.

There's a pile of rags on the floor. Flowery rags. Mrs Black Lady's trying to pick them up.

No. Not rags... an old lady. On the floor. Do I know her?

'Oh dear, Freida. Well, never mind. I'll send someone to clean you up. You stay there, there's a good girl.' Mrs Black Lady looks over my head. 'Anyone around? Ah, Mishka!'

A blue lady. A shrimp.

'Freida's had a little accident. Would you mind? Thanks. Oh, and this is Doris, our new lady. We're doing the grand tour. Doris, this is Mishka. She'll be taking care of you too. Lots of new friends, I know. But you'll soon get to know us. Thanks a lot, Mishka. There we go, Freida. Mishka is going to get you all nice and clean again.'

I hang on to Sad Eyes. I know her from somewhere. Don't leave me alone. Who are these people? Do I know them? Where's George?

'And here's the lounge. And it's exercise time,' Mrs Black Lady says. 'Every Thursday, 2.30 p.m. Janette is our exercise person. She takes them through things. She's very good. There's a video, everything set to music. They remember music. But Janette talks them through as well. It seems to work better.'

People everywhere. Waving.

'And one and two. And one and two. And one and two.' Somebody stands up. Yellow Dress. I hate yellow. 'Not now, Dulcie. Keep your dress on just now, honey. Listen. Hear the music? Now, lift your arms, everybody. Right one first. There we go. Right arm, Jacob. Well done. And lift and drop, and lift and drop. Very good. Keep going. And lift and drop, and lift and drop. Very *good*! Now, left arm. And lift and drop, and lift and drop. Only one arm at a time, Dulcie. Very good. And lift and drop. And rest. OK, we're going to bend at the knee now. One leg then the other one. Ready? Right one first. Right leg, Jacob... no, *right* one. This one. OK, everybody? And bend and stretch, and bend and stretch. No, Harriet, Daisy can do it by herself, there's a good girl.'

Everybody's moving.

'Take me home.'

'Connie, the doctor's here.'

'Oh, excuse me again. I'm so sorry about this.'

'Let's go somewhere quiet, shall we, Mum?' Sad Eyes. I know her... she puts her hand under my arm.

There's a big red chair like...

'You sit there. It'll settle down soon. It won't seem so bad when you know your way around, know the people. Close your eyes, listen to the music.'

'And one and two. And one and two.'

Nice chair like... Grandpapa... '*Once upon a time...*

Grandpapa is holding out his hand. It's all gnarled and grey.

There's another hand on my back guiding me towards him. I don't like it. He smells.

'*Come closer, my dear. What a pretty little thing. So like your mamma at that age. Come and let Grandpapa tell you stories about your mamma.*'

The hand insists.

'*Once upon a time there was a little girl. Her name was Hannah. She had big grey eyes and lots of lovely blonde curls and...*'

'Mum, wake up. Connie's going to take us to the dining room now.'

'And here we are,' Mrs Black Lady says. 'All meals are taken in here. We rotate the residents so that they don't develop little cliques or get stuck with the same faces.'

Lots of tables. Must be a party.

She presses buttons. The door opens.

'Are there locks on all the doors?' She's hoarse. She's whispering.

'On the outside ones, yes. For everyone's protection.'

Sad Eyes looks old. Is she going to cry?

'Right, so this is the sun-room. Why don't you have a little bit of quiet together-time. And then, when you're ready, we'll do the paperwork. I'll get a cup of tea sent out to you.'

Ah. Fresh air. Lovely.

'Oh, this is nice, isn't it, Mum? Like your conservatory. Look at these flower beds. I wonder if they let you help with the weeding. Maybe we could ask in a bit.'

A blue lady puts a tray on the table.

'Thank you so much. That's very kind,' Sad Eyes says.

Pretty cups. With saucers. Good. Flowers. Periwinkle blue. Like...

'And look, Garibaldi biscuits, Mum. Your favourite.'

'Do I know you?'

'Yes, Mum. I'm your daughter, Jessica.'

'Do you know Nelson Mandela?'

'No, I don't personally. But he's free now. He's fine.'

'Have you seen George?'

'Not today, no. Now, drink up your tea.'

It's warm. Peaceful.

He's late. Where is he? Ahh, there's the doorbell.

'Is that you, George? Hello?'

'Mrs Mannering?'

'Yes.'

'May we come in?'

Policemen? Here? In my house?

'Is it George?'

'I'm afraid so.'

...

He's stone cold. Blue. Eyes staring. Mouth open.
His shirt is wringing wet.
George?
George!

'No! No! No!'

'It's OK, Mum, you were only dreaming.'

'George?'

'Don't cry. Look, have your tea.'

It's cold.

'So. Here we are again.' Black Lady. 'Now, Doris, I need to have a little chat with your daughter. How about you come in here and watch television for a minute or two? There's a nice programme on about antiques.'

'I won't be a minute,' Sad Eyes whispers.

People everywhere. Who are they? Did I invite them?

Who's she? Why is she shouting? Who rang that bell? Why is he doing tha... Oh, naughty, naughty. Nice boys don't do that. Why is she standing there? Did I invite her? Is she waiting for me? Why is she shouting? Can I help you?

'OK, Betty.' It's a blue lady. 'Enough. You sit down here and hush for a bit. You're giving everybody a headache with all this shouting.'

Sad Eyes pushes me into a chair.

'Hello?' Red Hair. Funny voice. Right beside me.

'Do I know you?'

'My name, it is Jenica. I come from Ukraine.'

Shouting. Who's shouting?

'Betty! Betty! Shht! Sorry, Doris. Sometime Betty let off steam. We see TV, yes? Then not hear Betty.'

'*Ten pounds,*' the man says, waving his arm. '*Fifteen. Twenty. Twenty at the back of the room. Any advance on twenty? Twenty-five. New bidder. Do I see thirty? Thirty anywhere? Last chance. Selling for twenty-five.*'

Bang!

Who did that?

'*Lot 254. A bronze nude. Charming little piece this, gentlemen. Let's start the bidding at eighty pounds. Do I see ninety anywhere? Thank you, sir. Ninety pounds. A hundred. And ten. And twenty. And thirty. And forty. One hundred and fifty pounds. It's against you, sir. With the gentleman in the tweed jacket. Going once. Going twice.*'

Bang!

Who did that?

'Mum, I'm back. It's time to go up to your room. Dr Griffiths wants to see you and I have to see Connie again before I go, so up you come.'

'Take me home.'

Who's this?

'Do I know you? Did I invite you? Would you like a cup of tea?'

He's holding out both his hands. He's smiling.

I smile.

'You don't actually know me but I'm here to introduce myself. My name's Mark Griffiths. I'm one of the doctors here and it's my job to take care of you.'

A doctor. He'll know. 'Where's George?'

'He's not here right now. I'm Dr Griffiths. So, how are you today, Doris?'

'Fine. Thank you. I'm fine.'

'Do you know who I am, Doris?'

'No. Did I invite you?'

'Where are you now, Doris?'

'46 Clerk Street.'

'And what year is it?'

'1914–18.'

'And who's the prime minister?'

'Do I know you?'

'We're getting there!'

'Would you like some tea?'

'In a bit. Who's the prime minister, Doris?'

'Do you know?'

'I do. Do you?'

'I do.'

'No flies on you, I can see! Do you know where you are?'

'Never talk to strangers.'

'But I'm not a stranger now, Doris. I'm your doctor. So you can talk to me. I'm only trying to help you. I'm Dr Griffiths. Who am I?'

'Doris Elizabeth Fenton.'

'Well done. And who did you marry?'

'George.'

'Very good! And did you and George have any children?'

'Where's George?'

'Your children. Can you tell me their names?'

'What time is it? Mustn't be late.'

'Right. The children… Jessica, maybe?'

'No. They don't come any more.'

'Adeline?'

'At school. She's at school. Is it time?'

'OK. What year were you born, Doris?'

'You're as old as you feel.'

'Well said! Just the kind of answer my Aunty Mima would give! Well done.'

He smiles. I smile. Kind eyes. Hairs in his nose. I don't like hai…

'He's hiding,' I whisper.

'Who's hiding?' he whispers back.

'George.'

'Is he indeed?' He leans back, stops whispering. 'I think we'll start you on some medicine to help you to be happy. OK?'

'They're trying to poison me.'

I whisper it, so they won't hear.

'Are they?'

'Mamma will be cross.'

The door opens. He stops looking at me. I'm free.

'Oh, I'm sorry. I didn't mean to interrupt.' It's Sad Eyes.

'Ah, Mrs Burden. Come in, come in. It's fine. I'm almost finished here anyway. Your mum's been very helpful. We've had a good chat.'

She makes a funny noise.

'Right, I'll leave you two to settle in and I'll see you around.'

She's stroking my hand. Who is she? Is she from the television?

'You do understand, don't you? It's for the best. You'll be safe here. I'll come and see you often. And maybe when James is free we could take you out. That'd be nice, wouldn't it? And I can bring you some of your favourite things. Gorgonzola. And walnuts. Chocolate mousse. Aunty Jean's bun loaf. And apple strudel...'

'Did I hear strudel?'

'James! Oh, how lovely to see you!' She's hugging this big man.

'I can't let my favourite Gran move house and not pop in to say hello, now can I? How're you doing? Can I have a kiss?'

His bristles are scratchy. He smells of something nice. Reminds me of...

'How about a proper hug for your favourite grandson?'

I want to go home now.

'So this is your room. *Very* nice. And look at your view. Brilliant. The Pentlands. Quite like old times.'

'It *is* nice, isn't it?' Sad Eyes isn't sad now.

'Excellent. Looks new.'

'It's all just been redecorated. New curtains, new carpet. Everything.'

'Great. And here's a little something to welcome you to your new home, Gran. Your favourites. Freesias.'

'That was kind.'

'She'll probably eat them for breakfast!'

I watch them. I think I know him. He's nice.

'So. What have you been up to today?' he smiles at me.

'Did I…'

'Since we got here?' Sad Eyes interrupts me. 'Stuffed a good scarf down the loo, locked ourselves in the toilet, broken a china cup… the usual.'

He shakes his head. 'Well, at least they won't think you got her here under false pretences.'

'Somehow I doubt that. Although the doctor said he had a nice chat with her.'

Somebody's tapping on the door.

'George?'

Mr Nice-Smell gets up. Opens the door.

'Well, hello. This is Doris Mannering's mansion. I'm her butler, James. How may I help you?'

'Well, that's a first! Hi. I'm Sue. And I'm one of the carers. I've come to see if Doris is ready for supper.'

'D'you hear that, Gran? You've been invited out to supper. Perfect. You go off to your banquet, and us poor serfs will head off for mince and tatties, yeah?'

Suddenly Sad Eyes is holding me tight. 'I love you, Mum. I really do love you. And I'll come and see you often.' She's all trembly.

'So, shall we go?' the blue lady says. She sticks out her elbow and pulls my hand through.

'Bye, Gran. Have fun. See you.' Mr Nice-Smell blows a kiss. He's smiling. I smile.

The old one's eyes are weeping. Sad. I know her.

'See you!' The blue lady isn't pushing me. The floor's all soft. I smell…

'Macaroni cheese, tonight. Smells good, eh? Nice enough to eat.'

Chapter 14
A month earlier

HE'S BACK! I SAW him. Plain as day.

She can scoff all she likes, I *know* he's there. In the corner. I *saw* him. Humming.

'It's all right, Mum,' she says in that patronising voice, as if I'm a child. 'It's only Jeremy Paxman. He can't hurt you. It's only the TV. There we are, look. All gone.'

It's not. I know it's not.

What's that noise? Ringing. Who's that?

'Hello, James. Come on in. Gran will be so pleased to see you.'

'How is she today?' It's a big voice. Do I know him? Did I invite him?

'Twitchy. And quite aggressive.'

'Did the doctor come this morning?'

'He did indeed.'

'And?'

'He agrees. She does need to go. Definitely.'

'Hallelujah! So you told him then?'

'Well...'

'About the night-time antics? Coming at you with a knife? Smashing the plates? Yes? Tell me you did, Mum.'

'Sort of. But I...'

'She *has* to go. You can't keep this up. She's a danger to herself as well as to you.'

'I know. It's just, I feel as if I'm letting her down.'

'That's rubbish and you know it.'

'Let's not talk about it right now. She's dozing in the living room. You pop in and see her and I'll make the tea.'

He fills the doorway. Do I know him?

'Well, hello, hello, hello! Look at you. Aren't you the glamour puss today?'

He flops onto a seat and leans close to whisper, 'So have you been behaving yourself?'

'Did I invite you?'

'No, as it happens, I invited myself. No manners, the up-and-coming generation, huh? Breezing in all unannounced and uninvited. I don't know what the world's coming to.'

I watch him out of the very edge of my eye. Did he come out of the corner? Did he see... you know? Are they plotting?

'You need to write a letter. Tell the Queen. It's Frank.'

'No, Gran. I'm James, not Frank. Your grandson. James.'

'James.'

'I like your new skirt. Very trendy.'

What's that noise? Clinking.

'A pyjama jacket on her legs is the least of my worries,' she says, putting the tray down.

No doilies. I should pour the tea.

'So what else have you two girls been up to today... what have you done to your arm, Mum?'

'Shsh.' She flicks her eyes at me. Why is she holding her arm in her hand like that? That's no way to pour the tea. I should do it. 'She doesn't mean to.'

'Here, let me. You need to get that looked at.' Mr Nice-Smell puts her into the chair. Is she going to cry?

He pours the tea.

'D'you want me to ring The Morningside for you?'

'No. I'll do it. Just give me time.'

'Mother! You've given this thing *time* for the past however many years. If you can't do it, I will.'

'No, I will, James. I will.'

'Have you talked to her about it?'

'I've tried.'

'She did it,' I tell him.

'Did what?'

'The whole wedding. All that food!'

'Did she indeed. Who's "she"?'

'Princess Di.'

'Wow.'

'Did I invite you?' I ask him. Did I?

'No, Gran. But listen, I can come and visit you anywhere, can't I?'

'*James!*' Why is she shouting?

I've got to get away. I hate shouting.

He's strong. He's got me. Help!

'Let me *go*!'

'Now, steady on. I'm a lot bigger than Mum. You can't escape from me, so just you calm down, huh, and we'll talk about this rationally.'

'No, we will *not*!' she says. She's cross. She reminds me of... What have I done? Am I in trouble?

'Please, Papa. I'm sorry.'

'I'll let you go if you promise to behave, OK? Right. That's better.'

'See what you've done now!' she says.

'I'm sorry. But you've got to move on this before something tragic happens. You'd never forgive yourself.'

'I know. And I will.'

'When? *When* will you?'

'Tomorrow.'

'Promise?'

'I will.'

'Why don't you let me do it for you? I could go there after work today and check availability and everything in person.'

She shakes her head.

'No, it's something I have to do myself.'

'Well then, phone *now* to book a time. I'll come and stay with Gran.'

He follows her out.

It's peaceful. Nobody shouting. Just the hum of…

Humming. The whole shed's humming. I love the sound.

It's like the pulse of the farm. Throbbing. Carrying the life-blood. The milk froths into the tubes, the tension goes out of the udders, the veins stop bulging fit to burst.

From where I'm crouched I can see all the bony bums of the cows all pointing the same way, tails swishing occasionally, the sound of chomping. A tail lifts; dung splatters the concrete, the sickly smell rising above the disinfectant Uncle Frank scrubbed into the ground only two hours ago. His big muscles contract and extend, his hobnail boots clatter on the ground. The stiff brush scuffs the water and the milk and the dung out of the cracks as he 'puts his back into it'. If a job's worth doing, it's worth doing well. He doesn't stop until it's all hosed down and you can't see any animals have ever been in here.

Uncle Frank learned the hard way, Mamma says. Farming's not in his blood. It's in Aunt Annie's blood, though.

'Love me, love my cows,' Papa says. I hear him. Laughing. I'm up in the hay loft; they don't know.

'Aye. You'll not prise our Annie from her farm for love nor money. No, that lassie's bin rising at 5 since she were 10-year-old. Aye, that she has. She's maybe no oil painting, but she knows cows inside out and back to front like they were her bairns. Many's the time she's coaxed one of 'em to drop a calf while the menfolk stood back shaking their heads. Up to her armpits inside 'em. It's all in a day's work for our Annie. And up she'd get every hour to feed that little mite like it was the fullness o' her own milk that waked her. And you'll not get a faster worker this side o' Berwick and that's a fact. She'll have the milking done and the place all scrubbed neat as a pin, and

still have the bacon and sausage on the table afore eight. Aye, she's a good lass. She'll make your Frank a good wife. But it'll be on her terms, mind. The farm goes wi' her.'

...

Uncle Frank's wedding is so noisy.

He's old. Approaching 40, Mamma says. I don't ever want to be that old.

I'm so hungry. But they keep talking. Funny accents, funny smells, stories about animals – jokes that make the men-folk roar with laughter. Mamma tuts. Several times. She tweaks the sash of my brand new white dress with the blue bolero.

'Just you close your ears, Doris.'

It goes on and on. After the cake and everything. I wish I could go home. It's boring.

...

Holiday times we go to the farm so's we get to 'know about the country'. The kittens are my favourites. Outside they are, all weathers. They're 'working animals,' Aunt Annie says, 'not for petting.' But the kittens, well, catch them with their eyes still sewn up and you can carry them round in your pocket and stroke their little bodies and feel the purring right into the middle of your tummy, it's that gorgeous.

And we get to scamper round outside all day too, like the kittens. Reuben and Jack, they're allowed to drive the tractor. Imagine! The wheels are so big they're nearly as high as Uncle Frank. He puts the boys on his lap and hollers at them to grab hold of the steering wheel with two hands and off they go bumping all over the fields, squealing and shouting and feeling like regular farmers. Sydney and Derek and me, we aren't allowed near the big machines but we get to feed the chickens and pick up the eggs for Aunt Annie.

...

The cows skitter over the yard, their hooves all clickety clack on the stone, going into the milking parlour like they're on invisible ropes, knowing where to stand. Like they're in a hurry to be emptied out. And I'd be in a hurry too, lugging all those bottles of milk inside my udder – if I was a cow, I mean.

Going into the milking shed's my secret. Sydney or Derek, they'd only spoil it, getting bored. I just want to watch that milk being sucked out.

Uncle Frank likes udders. He strokes them, washes them, holds them. Even when they're all clipped up and the milk's racing down the tubes, he walks up and down feeling one after the other, smiling a funny kind of smile. Pleased.

'You feel that, Doris. See. Give me your hand. Feel how hard it is all full up of milk. And the nipple, see, pink and long. Just right for a baby's mouth. And we pop the nipples in here like that and we switch on and she loves it. See she's smiling now. Aren't you, Constance, old girl? She loves it. And that's why she comes dancing in here twice a day. She knows Uncle Frank will make her feel like a princess. Don't you, my beauty?'

I like that. Watching the cows loving it. Seeing all that milk.

...

'And look at this one, Doris.'

No! You're spoiling it! Leave me alone, Uncle Frank. You can't!

Now I'll never get to drive the tractor.

Who put this thing on me? You can't drive tractors in pyjamas! Don't they know anything?

I hear them whispering. I know they're plotting.

'She isn't necessarily asleep.'

'What kinds of things?'

'All dressed up in loads of jumpers and coats, it was a devil of a job to get them off her... she screams the place down. God knows what the neighbours think. A couple of nights ago I woke to this *apparition* beside my bed, stark naked, staring down at me. I didn't know what she was going to do.'

'Sounds like the mad woman in *Jane Eyre*. I don't know how you've tolerated it all this time. A break is long, long overdue. I know I make a joke of it but I do sympathise. Really I do.'

'I know. Sorry if I'm snappy sometimes... I'm so *tired.*'

'That's a strong contender for the understatement-of-the-century prize! By the way, the new post-it on the fridge: "*This is a fridge. It's only for food. It's cold inside.*" And the story is?'

'Oh, she only squeezed a whole tube of toothpaste into the mug she keeps her teeth in, diluted it with some bath oil – and then emptied it onto a meringue gateau I'd put on the top shelf. And then jammed the door open.'

'I hope it wasn't something you'd slaved over for hours.'

'My days of slaving over any food are long gone. I haven't got the energy.'

'Well, I'm looking forward to a return of the old Mum, best apple pie maker in the whole of the UK – once Gran's settled. I'll give you a day or two to recover first but then I'm expecting great things. But I'd better scoot. I'll be here at 9.15 in the morning.'

'Bless you, James.'

'Right. I'm off for now, Gran. You behave for Jessica, now.'

'You've got to get me out of here.' I hiss in his ear so they won't hear.

'I will. I promise. Very soon. It's all arranged.'

Chapter 15
A year earlier

WHAT AM I doing here? I don't like this place. They've kidnapped me.

They got Uncle Stanley, I know. Poor Uncle Stanley. Smart in his uniform. Off to war. But they got him.

He's in the albums. She makes me look. I hate it.

'Who's this? Remember him? Which one's that? Tell me about him. Remember when you...'

Questions. Always questions.

'Who's the prime minister?' 'What year is it?' 'Where do you live?' 'When were you born?'

Tricks.

'Going to ask you again later on.'

She made me sit there and go through it. *Made* me!

Stupid questions. 'Where are you now?' 'What was that address I asked you to remember?' It's so exhausting.

'Is she asleep?'

'I'm not sure. Do we have to keep putting her through all this?'

'The point of these tests is to see if there's any change, Mrs Burden.'

'And is there?'

'I'm afraid there's been a steady deterioration now over the last three tests. In her memory and her mental agility.'

'She *tried* to keep her brain active. Crosswords, reading, Sudoku.'

The light makes me squint.

Where's my purse? Who's taken it? They're always taking things.

'Where's my purse?'

'Who knows?'

'They've stolen it.'

'Nobody's stolen it. It's probably where you last put it, but that might be anywhere under the sun and quite frankly, I have better things to do than hunt for your dratted purse!'

'Where's my purse?'

'For goodness' sake, Mother!'

'I need to go home.'

'You know, you really are infuriating. Whenever the doctor or the nurse are here, you smile and behave as if butter wouldn't melt in your mouth, but the minute they go – oh, what's the use!'

'I need to get my purse? It's Reuben. Reuben's got it.'

'Reuben's dead.'

'Have you got my purse?'

'I don't know where your purse is! I don't *care* where it is! Pandora's coming today and I have so much to do, I don't know where to start. So either sit there and be quiet, or I shall have to lock you in your room again. D'you hear me?'

There's no need to shout. Why is she shouting? What have I done?

'And throw away the key.' Why is she whispering? She's plotting. I knew it.

'Where's my purse?'

It's quiet in here. But I don't like it. Let me out.

The handle rattles. Why won't it open?

'Let me out. Help!'

'It's for your own good. You're driving me to distraction and any minute now I shall do something dreadful if you don't shut up!'

'Where's my purse?'

Nothing.

'Where's my purse?'

Nothing.

'My purse.'

Nothing. It's hot in here.

The attic's cramped and hot. And smells of dust. But I don't care. I want to see all these treasures before they go.

I sneak a look at Mamma. Is she cross? Or sad? I think it's sad. 'Cos she's throwing away Grandmamma's things. And 'cos her mamma's dead.

But this is like... history in boxes. Better history than we get at school. Much better. Specially when Mamma tells me all about life back then, when she was a girl. First it was the treadle sewing machine, then the rocking horse, and the case with the gold letters on it...

But the dress is the best thing of all. Mamma smooths the folds like it's a cat or something. The spangles glint in the light. I love all the little pleats on the sleeves, the gorgeous black beads.

'It belonged to your grandmother when she was a young lady. May, her name was,' Mamma says, crying inside but not outside.

'It's a duchess dress,' I whisper.

'Well, your grandmamma was almost a duchess. Her father owned a lot of land, and they lived in a very grand house, with servants.'

'My grandmamma?'

'Yes. And it was all to be hers one day. You see, May's father, your great-grandfather, didn't have a son to inherit it; he only had daughters. Two daughters. And the eldest one, Augusta, died when she was only six months old, so Grandmamma was

the only surviving child.'

'Like in the fairy stories.'

'Yes. And like in the fairy stories she ran away. She left it all behind.'

'Why?'

'Because she fell in love with a poor man. A minister's son. Albert Edward Hawksworth – Bertie.'

'Like Queen Victoria.'

'Except that Victoria's Albert was a prince and May's Bertie was as poor as a church mouse.'

'She must have loved him very much. It is like a fairy story.'

'But this story really did happen. May married Bertie. And after a while they had a little girl. And that was me! And we have the dress to remind us that she was once a very grand lady.' She touches the black skirt. Her fingers are like feathers. *'This was the only dress she took with her. She wasn't going to need clothes like this once she was married to her Bertie.'*

'Didn't she ever wear it again?'

'Only once – on her wedding day. There was no one there to see her except Bertie and the minister who married them. After that she packed it away in a case and never looked at it again. And when I was seven, the same age you are now, she showed it to me and told me this story.'

It feels like we're in a church now. Nobody speaking. Looking at the dress, thinking about that wedding with nobody there.

The squeak wakes me. They've come for me. Help!

'You lock her in?'

'It's for her own safety. I can't have her wandering off as soon as my back's turned. Turning on the gas, leaving taps running, grabbing knives, boiling kettles dry, striking matches – you name it, she's done it.'

The door's opening. Two women stare in. The old one... I know her. And... who's that? Did I invite her?

'Oh *Mum*!' The young one wrinkles up her nose.

'I know,' the old one mutters.

'It's not *sanitary*! You can't live like this.'

'Hello. Do I know you?'

'You should do. I'm Pandora. You've known me all my life.'

'Did I invite you?'

'No, Gran. This is Mum's home.'

'Pandora's brought her two little ones, Mum. Let's get you freshened up and then we'll go down and see them, shall we?'

Don't! Don't do that! Leave me alone.

'Open your legs wider. No, wider. It's only me, Mum. No, don't put your hands in there. Mother! *Don't!* Look, you hold onto this rail. Two hands. And open your legs for me... no! Don't do that! Stop it! You're hurting me. *Please!*'

'Gran! Stop it! Let go of Mum's hair.' The other one's grabbing me. 'Now look what you've done! You've made her cry.'

'I'm not crying, Pandora. She pulled my hair, that's what made my eyes water. She doesn't mean it. She doesn't know what she's doing.'

'Oh, *Mum*. You shouldn't have to put up with this.'

There are two children in the room.

'This is Karah and this is Max. Say, "Hello, Granny D".'

'Hello, Granny D.'

'Hello.'

'Brilliant. Well done, Mum. Now, you come and sit over here in your special chair. You have a wee chat with Pandora and I'll get us all a drink.'

'Karah's learning to play the flute, Gran. Remember Dad used to play the oboe? Well, the flute's something like it.'

'It is *not*!' the girl on the floor says. 'The oboe's *gross*! I wouldn't be seen dead with an oboe.'

'I know, darling. But Granny D...'

'I thought you said she...'

'Shsh, Karah. Not in front of her, OK?'

'And Max is in a rugby team. He's very good.'

'He is *not*!' Spitting.

The old woman comes in, carrying things.

'Here we are then, a nice cup of tea. I'll put yours over here till it cools a bit, Mother. Karah, mango juice, dear? Max? And how about a chocolate biscuit?'

'Oh, you remembered. Mango. Max's favourite. Thanks, Mum.'

Everybody's drinking. *Whhssht. It's poison!*

Chocolate, mm. I like chocolate.

'Oh, look at you!' Sad Eyes grabs my arm. 'I knew I shouldn't have. Give me your hand. No! Don't do that. What a mess. There we go, let's wipe that all off your hair. Pandora, could you fetch her a plain Rich Tea, from the biscuit barrel on the first shelf in the kitchen?'

The children are snorting. *Poison.* I knew it.

'There you are, Gran. A biscuit. Put it straight in your mouth.'

Do I know her? Pan…?

'Children, why don't you go outside and play in the garden for a while. I want to talk to Nana for a bit.'

They're still making weird noises. Not dead yet.

The little one shuts the door hard.

I close my eyes.

'Is she asleep? Can we go somewhere?'

'I can't leave her, Pandora. There's no saying what she'll get up to when she's in this kind of mood.'

'Mum, you *have* to get help.'

'It only makes her worse. She didn't like strangers in the house. She needs routine. And familiar faces.'

'What about a day centre or something?'

'We tried that. She hated it. They had to prise her off me. It was horrible. And when they did get her inside – by force really – she kept trying to run away. And she was much worse at home too. It was like she was scared the whole time they were going to take her away. It simply wasn't worth the hassle.'

'Could they maybe give her something? Make her drowsy?'

'They aren't keen on sedating them.'

'Why ever not? I'd have thought it'd be preferable from *her* point of view to be out of it.'

'Sedatives can have side effects too – some of them a bit like dementia. And anyway we don't know if Gran would consent to them if she knew what they were.'

'You mean – you aren't *serious*?'

'What d'you mean?'

'*Mum!* Look at her! You're doing everything else for her. Surely, if she's out of control, you have the right to decide she needs sedated. You need a life, too.'

'But that's exactly why they don't like to do it. Putting the interests of the carer above the patient's. It wouldn't be morally right.'

'What nonsense! If *you're* totally exhausted and depressed and unable to think straight, surely that's not in her best interests?'

'Will you pass that blanket to Charles and Diana. Please. Charles and Diana,' I say.

'Have your tea, Mum.'

Mm. Nice. Warm. Lets me think. Quiet.

Reuben, Jack and Sydney are hiding.

'*Coming, ready or not!*'

It's Derek's turn to be seeker.

He turns round, his eyes darting from side to side in case the boys leap out at him straight away. They won't though. I can see them all from the tree house. They're pelting away as hard as their much longer legs will carry them.

Derek wanders off. It's only a few minutes and he's back.

'*Doris, have you seen the others?*'

'*Nope.*' *He looks small and frightened down there, all on his own.* '*Why don't you come up here an' play with me instead?*'

His pudgy little fingers are white with the effort of hanging on to the ladder into the tree house. He flops down on my cushion – the one I keep just for me. The dolls aren't allowed to use it.

'Want a drink?' I say.

'Yeeah!' His eyes sparkle.

'Whooosh. There you are. It's dandelion an' burdock. Mind you don't spill it on my cushion,' I say fiercely, handing him a chipped china cup from my second-best tea-set.

Derek bursts into tears.

'What's up?' I say. He can be a pest sometimes.

'It's all empty!' he wails.

'Course it is. It's pretend.*'*

'But I'm thirsty!' he wails.

'Go home then.'

'Will you come with me? So Reuben an' them won't jump out at me.'

He has this daft idea that I can protect him from his three older brothers. As if!

I sigh. I'd better. Mum always says we have to look after the little ones. Only the boys reckon that's me, not them. I was having fun too partying with all the dolls and everything. All on my own, nobody to laugh at me. 'Cos the boys do scoff – specially Sydney. Two things he really despises: sissies and school. He told me: books are a punishment God thought up. And right now Sydney's into punishment. Ever since Beatrice came he's had more than his share of it.

...

Mamma sighs. 'Yes, your Alicia's right, sadly. I'm afraid Sydney was sent home from school again this week but this kind of behaviour is very much out of character. He's never been in trouble like this before.'

'Boys will be boys, Mrs Fenton. And all I can say is, I'm glad all mine are girls,' says Mrs McFilligree from next door. She folds her arms under her bosom, gives it a hoist, like she does. I can see her through all the twigs and leaves, but they can't see me sitting inside the hedge. Not if I keep ever so still.

'I've had four boys, Mrs McFilligree, as well as two girls,' Mamma sounds sharp, like her corset is chafing, 'And both have their pluses and minuses. But I can tell you this is more than being a boy. Something troubles him, that I know. Something or someone.'

'Is it the baby? Only when my youngest was born the next one up took to tantrums and screaming and all sorts. It took a good leathering to bring her to her senses.'

'Yes, but you see Sydney isn't the next one up. That's Derek. Four years he's been the baby but he adores his baby sister. It's Sydney who's the trouble. He's the third one. And he's eight, going on nine.'

'Eight? Old enough to know what's what, I'd say.'

And then... Atttishoo. It comes before I even know it's laying eggs inside my nose.

'Doris! Come out of there. At once!'

I'm glad Mamma isn't Mrs McFilligree. I'd have been leathered sure enough.

'Off to bed, young lady. And if I ever catch you...'

I cry hard enough 'cos of missing my tea, never mind leathering.

And then there was the rat.

...

'Sydney Fenton!' Mamma roars. 'You will be the death of me! What on earth possessed you to take Barnaby to school in the first place?'

Now usually Sydney knows you have to act like you're sorry even when you aren't deep down inside, but this time is he acting? No, sir! He is not! He's totally indignant, that's what.

'Mrs Gussman was tellin' us about rats. They started the plague an' it was dead interestin'. But some of the girls were like eeuuuuch an' I thought if they could see Barnaby...'

'...you'd convert them! Sydney, Sydney, Sydney,' Mamma says, shaking her head till her curls come unstuck. 'What am I going to do with you? Poor Mrs Gussman's had half the parents of the children in your class up in arms. I despair of you. Really

I do. Whatever will you think up next?'

Mamma's done a fair amount of despairing lately. As far as Sydney's concerned.

This time she's mad as fire! I can hear Sydney's yells from here. Papa's giving him a real skelping. And it must be bad to burn down the pampas grass 'cos Mamma doesn't usually tell Papa. She can slap hard enough all on her own. But everybody in our house knows you don't touch matches. He reckons he didn't mean to make a blaze, only light one little strand. But Mamma says it's been a totally dry summer and he should've known it would go up like a bonfire. The wonder of it was he didn't kill himself too, she says. And that's when she gives him a hug that swallows him up. Only she looks like she knows she shouldn't oughta.

'Muummy! Karah won't let me have a go on the swing.'

'Oh Max! Look what you've done. You've woken Granny D.'

'But Karah's being mean.'

'Children, come upstairs and play. Mum, here's your book about the royal family. Look, there's the Queen, visiting America. Doesn't she look lovely? And who's this? The Duke of Gloucester, and the Duchess. You could have told me that, couldn't you?'

'I never knew that,' the young one says.

'Oh yes, Gran was always very keen on the royals.'

'I'm bored. Can we go now?' It's a little girl. What's she doing here?

'I'm coming,' Sad Eyes says. 'Keep an eye on Gran, Pandora. Look, Mum, there's the Queen. Wearing your favourite colour. Powder blue. Lovely. Why don't you tell Pandora all about the time you made a dress like the Queen's, eh?'

'You made a dress, Gran?'

'Did I invite you? Have you got my purse?'

'No. Look here's Prince Andrew. And Edward...'

I'm sleepy...

Here's Sad Eyes.

'Right. A fresh cup, Pandora?'

'No, thanks. I'm not really a tea drinker.'

'Coffee then?'

'No. I'm not keen on instant. Actually, we'd better be going. I only popped in to see how you were doing. I'm having my hair done at 4.30 and I need to get the children to Claire's before that. We'll come for longer next time.' She opens the door. 'Karah! Max! Time to go.'

'Ohh, Mummy! I don't want to go yet. Can I stay with Nana?'

'Shsh. It's too noisy for Granny D. Let's go out into the hall. Say goodbye to her, and then out we go.'

'Goodbye, Granny D.'

'Bye, Gran. See you soon.'

'I'll be back in two ticks, Mum.'

Lovely. Nobody here.

It's dark in the corner. Something's humming.

Is that you, Frank? Are you there? Go away.

I'll close my eyes. I don't want to see it.

The shed's humming. Uncle Frank is getting it out…

No! I don't want to! I don't want to.

'Mum! Mum! It's OK. You're quite safe.' Sad Eyes pats my arm.

'Don't let him get me!'

'There's nobody here, only you and me. Wasn't it nice of Pandora to call in to see us? Shame they couldn't stay longer.'

Her sigh whispers against my cheek like the edge of a cow's tail.

Chapter 16

Eighteen months earlier

I MUST FIND THEM. It's important. I know it is. But where are they? I put them in a special place. Ahh. Fresh air. Lovely.

'Oh Mum. I can't have you all muddy and wet today, you've got a visitor coming to see you. Come on back inside.'

'Beatrice?'

'No, Mum. I'm Jessica.'

'This is my garden.'

'Yes, it is. But I'm living with you right now. Come on. There we go, back in your own chair. Right beside the photograph of Dad. Remember? George? Your husband? See. There he is.'

That's not George. He's too old.

He'll come out when she's gone. I know he will. He was always shy, George.

'Here's one of your favourite books. Prince Charles and Lady Di on their wedding day. I'll be back in a minute with your drink.'

Lady Di. Lady Di.

What's all that stuff round her? What a mess. Why don't they tidy her up?

Pretty face. Like... Beatrice.

'Please, Papa. Please don't be cross with him.'

'Stay out of this, Doris. I will not have any son of mine

scaring little girls out of their minds.'

'But, Papa, it wasn't nearly as bad as Bea's making out.'

'She's years younger than you, Reuben. You should know to make allowances.

'But he thought I'd find the spider, not Bea. And I wouldn't have minded. I like it when he treats me like the boys.'

'Is this the truth, boy? Did you intend it for Doris?'

'Yes, Papa. And I'm sorry Bea got scared. I wouldn't do it to her. She's such a cry-baby. No fun in teasing her. But Doris, she's a sport. She doesn't mind.'

'And if I could think of things I'd do them back, Papa. Only I can never think of anything bad enough to scare Reuben.'

Papa half-smiles. 'Off you go then, Doris. I need to have a chat with your brother.'

...

'Thanks, kiddo,' Reuben says roughly. 'Only, I don't need you to fight my battles. Got that? I told Papa so, an' all.'

'But you *wouldn't* have told on Bea. I know you wouldn't. And if she hadn't made such a fuss, Papa wouldn't have known about that spider.'

He grins. 'Pretty life-like, huh? My mate, Barry, got it from a joke shop. I bet you'd have shrieked if you'd found it first.'

'Bet I wouldn't.'

'Course you would. But you wouldn't have gone crying to Papa. You're OK, Doris. For a girl!'

Reuben? Are you there?

'You all right, Mum?'

'Is Reuben here yet?'

'No. He's been dead years.'

No! Oh no. Not Reuben. My Reuben.

'Don't be sad. It was all a very long time ago. Here, why don't I pop a video on and you can watch it until your visitor comes. I must get things cleared up. See? Hyacinth Bucket. One of your favourites. You enjoy all the pickles she gets herself into.'

Where is it? They steal things in here. I know they do. I must keep them out.

'What on earth? Damn it! What have you done *now*? Come on. I need to get in. There's somebody coming to see you any minute now. So be a good girl, move whatever it is. Mum, please. I'll bring you some Ovaltine if you let me in.'

'Where's my purse?'

'Here. You'll need to open the door so I can give it to you.'

'That's not my purse.'

'Yes, it is. Listen. Hear the money in it.'

'I need the toilet.'

'No, Mum. You don't. You can't. You've been eight times at least this morning.'

What's that? Ringing.

'Oh no!' she wails. 'There he is and look at us! Right. Sit down, Mother. Sit! And don't move while I get the door.'

I hear her.

'Hello.'

'Hello. Mrs Burden? I'm Ray Coulthard. I think you're expecting me?'

'Yes. Please, do come in. I'm sorry, we're in a terrible mess. I'm not usually as bad as this. Mother's been playing up this morning and now she's shut herself in, and barricaded the door with something.'

'Don't worry on my account. I'm not here to see the house, just your mother. And I know all about them playing up, believe me.'

I want to see who it is. Who put that there?

'She wouldn't do it when I asked...'

'Don't worry. I know.'

'I'm so sorry about the mess. But please, do go in. This is my mother, Doris Mannering. Mum, this is Mr Coulthard. He's come to chat to you.'

'Hello, Mrs Mannering. May I sit beside you?'

'Would you like a coffee?' she says.

'That would be very nice. Milk, two sugars, please. And what about you, Mrs Mannering? Will you join me in a coffee?'

'Did I invite you?'

'No. I've come to see how you're getting on.'

'That's nice.'

'So we'll both have a coffee, then, yes?'

'Thank you,' I say. The one I know is watching. 'Don't forget the serviettes,' I tell her. 'And the silver tongs.'

She shoots me a look. But then she's gone.

He gets out a paper thing. He smiles.

'Right. Do you know what year it is, Mrs Mannering?'

'2000 and... 2000 and...'

'And what day is it today?'

'Is it special? Is it my birthday?'

'No. I don't think so. How old are you? D'you remember?'

'Twenty-eight.'

'And who's the prime minister?'

'Winston Churchill.'

'Where are we now?'

'I don't know. Do you know?'

'Yes. We're in your home. In Bradley Drive.'

'Are we?'

'Is anyone else living here?'

'No, I live alone now.'

'Mrs Mannering, I want you to think of three objects, OK? Can you tell me what you're thinking about?'

'Nelson Mandela.'

She barges in, no knock, nothing. Rude.

'Sorry to take so long. I couldn't find the coffee. *Someone* had put it in the cupboard under the sink.'

'Smells wonderful,' he says.

She clatters around. He's waiting. I don't know what for.

'Thank you.' He takes a sip. 'Lovely. We'll leave it there for now. Concentrate on talking, yes? You were thinking of three objects.'

I'm waiting.

'You know, Mum. Things like coffee, cups, things like that.'

'Yes, please. No sugar.'

'Please, Mrs Burden... your mother...'

'Sorry.'

She goes away again.

'Would you like a coffee?' I ask him.

'I have one, thank you. Can you think of three things, Mrs Mannering?'

'I don't know.'

'What's this?'

'A cup.'

'And this?'

'A book.'

'And this?'

'A pencil? A pen?'

'Three things. A cup, a book, a pencil. Now can you tell me those three things?'

'Pencil.'

'Three things. Cup, book, pencil.'

'Cup, book, pencil.'

'Very good. Now, can you spell pencil backwards?'

'I don't know. Can you?'

'All right, I'm going to say something different. I want you to concentrate.'

'*Concentrate.*'

'Good. Here it is. No ifs, ands or buts. Can you say that?'

'I don't know. It's in the book. The red book.'

'Now I'm going to ask you to do a couple of things for me. Here's a teaspoon. I want you to pick it up, and place it on the saucer.'

The coffee's almost cold. I give it to him.

'Now I'd like you to read what it says on this piece of paper and then do what it says.'

It says, *clap your hands.*

The coffee *is* too cold. He hasn't drunk it.

'Fine, that's it. Now you can relax while I talk to your daughter. You can listen and chip in if you want to ask anything or comment.' He smiles at me. I smile back. He gets up. Calls, 'Mrs Burden.'

He smiles at her. She doesn't smile.

'I'm sure you don't need me to point out the problem areas.'

The old lady darts looks at me, at him, at me.

'Do we have to do this in front of her? She does follow some things still.'

'Indeed. And it's important there's no suggestion of plotting behind her back.'

He smiles again. I smile.

'We're now at the stage where I think we need a more thorough and expert assessment. There's a significant deficit and from what you've told me, looking after your mother is putting a considerable strain on you and your relationship.'

She flashes me a look. Guilty. What has she done?

'It's been helpful for me to see your mother in her own home environment.'

'Actually, I've only recently come to stay in Mum's house. She was living on her own before. But sometimes I wonder, is it adding to her confusion? Me being here, I mean. She thinks she's living years ago when my father was alive. She's always calling for him.'

'Yes. That often happens. The past is much clearer than the present and she will have better recall of long-ago events than the things that happened this week. As I'm sure you're only too well aware.'

'Ahhh, you're awake again, Mrs Mannering. I was just going. Thank you so much for talking to me. Very nice to meet you.'

'Nice to meet you too. Would you like a coffee?'

His handshake is firm and warm. 'No, thank you.'

'I'll see Mr Coulthard out, Mum, and I'll be straight back.'

I can hear them. Out there. In my hall.

'I suppose she recited all the prime ministers since William Gladstone for you!'

'Not exactly.'

'And once you've gone and we're back to the two of us, she'll probably insist that *she's* the prime minister!'

'I know. It can be immensely frustrating. But I'll get my report off this week and hopefully the appointment will be with you in the next month or so. I would advise you to take any help the social people can provide. Caring for someone at this stage is exhausting and demoralising. And it does help if you can get away and do your own thing occasionally.'

'Thank you. It's good to talk to someone who understands.'

'Take care of yourself too, then.'

I must get that cake cut up. They'll be here any minute.

There it is. My favourite knife. Always the same one. It's in all the pictures.

I'll just... What's *she* doing in my kitchen?

'Mum! Put. The. Knife. Down. Please.'

'It's time. I must get it done.'

'Pop it on the table. There's a good girl.'

They'll be here any minute. I must get ready. Why does she stand there, right in the way?

'I can't let you... Mum, let go! Let go!'

She's hurting me. I must get away.

'Let. Go. Of. The Knife.'

Ohh. She's hurting me.

'For goodness' sake, Mother! You'll be the death of me.'

'I don't like you.'

Why is she crying? I don't like it.

'I don't like you.'

'You don't like *me*! Because of you *I'm* losing everything I care about. My home. My peace of mind. My freedom...' and then in a whisper, 'My love.'

I have to go now. I must get ready.

'Oh no, you don't! Didn't you hear me? Enough's enough. You are going to go to your room and I'm going to lock you in before I kill you with my bare hands. It's one thing after another. And I can't... I absolutely *can not* take any more.'

Her fingers dig in. It hurts.

'I don't like you.'

'And at this precise moment, I hate you,' she hisses.

I hear the key turn in the lock.

'George? Help. Please help me.'

The noise wakes me. Scraping.

It's the door. Someone's coming in. It's the old lady. Tears running down her cheeks.

'I'm so, so sorry, Mum. I didn't mean to hurt you. But I'm so tired. I didn't mean what I said. I do love you. Really I do. I know it's not your fault.'

I need the toilet.

Chapter 17
Two years earlier

SHE SIMPLY WALKS IN.

'Hello, Doris, how are you today?'

'Hello. I'm fine, thank you. Nice to see you. Have you come far?'

'I'm Lily, from next door, dear. Brought you a nice piece of sponge.'

'Thank you very much. That's very kind of you.'

'Is it OK if I come in for a minute? Take the weight off me feet.'

'Please come in. Nice to see you.'

She walks past me. KEEP THE DOOR SHUT the sticker says. I close the door.

PUT THE LIGHT OFF LAST THING. I flick the switch.

'Ahhh, that's better. Now, I can see you!' she says, smiling. 'I've been thinking. How would it be if I had a key, and then you could keep the door locked?'

'Thank you for calling.'

'Maybe I'll speak to Jessica, then, eh? Coffee? Shall I do the needful?'

She's in my kitchen. She's touching things. I'm sure they're my things. THIS IS THE KETTLE. HOT. BE CAREFUL. It *is* my kitchen. SUGAR. TEABAGS. COFFEE. OVALTINE. MARMITE. BISCUITS, it says. She's reading it. SPOONS. KNIVES. FORKS.

'Did I invite you?'

'No, dearie,' she laughs. 'I popped round. Like neighbours do. I'm Lily. Remember?'

'Thank you for calling. It's my favourite. I'll pop it in the kitchen.'

'You're welcome. Oh, it grieves me to see you come to this, I must say. You that was always so busy, looking after everybody, loads of visitors and everything. Sad.'

'We're going on holiday tomorrow. I must pack.'

'Are you? Well, that's nice. I'll see myself out and you mind and keep the door shut tight now.'

It's... it's... my daughter! She kisses me. She's pretty when she smiles.

'Mum, you look nice today. That cardigan suits you. So, all set? Our appointment's at 11. Nothing to worry about. It's just a wee check-up.'

'I want to go home now.'

'This is your home, Mum. Bradley Drive. Remember? You and George bought this house. We grew up here, didn't we?'

'He doesn't like it. He's cross.'

'Nobody's cross. We only want you to be safe. So let's get you to the toilet and then I'll take you down to the surgery.'

He's nice. 'My name's Dr Robartz. And I'm going to ask you a few questions.' Irish like... like... all stiff and starchy...

'Can you tell me your name?'

'Doris Elizabeth Fenton.'

'Well done. And where do you live, Doris Elizabeth Fenton?'

'Bradley Drive.'

'And do you know who I am?'

'You're the doctor.'

'And who's this lady?'

'My daughter.'

She splutters. He puts a finger to his lips.

'Please don't be cross,' I say.

The doctor leans towards me. 'Nobody's cross. But I want you to concentrate on me right now, Doris. Please. This way. Over here. That's right.'

I smile. He smiles back.

'What year is it?'

'2002.'

'What day is it?'

'I don't know. I haven't seen the newspaper.'

'Fair enough. One day seems much like another when you're in the house, doesn't it?'

'I'm not in the house.'

He laughs. '*Touché.*'

The one I know smiles. I smile at her. That's better.

'Do you know who the prime minister is, Doris?'

'Mrs Thatcher.'

'Right. Where are we now?'

'At the doctor's.'

Backwards and forwards it goes. Makes me dizzy. I want to go home.

'Well done, Doris. That's all for now. Thank you. You've done very well.'

He smiles. I smile. She isn't smiling. She looks sad.

'I'm sorry,' I say.

She pats my arm. 'It's not your fault. Nobody's blaming you.'

The doctor leans back in his chair.

'So is it... you know?' she says.

'Well, I can't say for sure.'

'How can you tell?'

'The only sure way is at post mortem. But MRI scans can give us indicators. And these cognitive tests along with the medical history.'

'Nobody seems to want to give it a label.'

'In the early stages I think most people are reluctant to do so. It's a condition that needs to be monitored over time. The people in our memory clinics can help us firm up the diagnosis and track the deterioration. But I think we've got a fairly classic picture of messages not transmitting properly in the brain – difficulties in remembering, making decisions, expressing thoughts, and communicating generally, understanding what other people are saying, finding her way around.'

'Don't get me wrong, I don't *want* to hear that's what it is. Only without a label, it's hard to explain to people.'

'I understand. You're in limbo. And that's why…' He swings his chair to face me. 'Doris, I'd like to refer you to a specialist. We aren't quite sure what treatment to give you, so we need somebody else to see you. That OK?'

'I'll have to ask George.'

'She insists she wants to stay in her own home. She was always adamant that she wouldn't live with any of us. But is that…?'

'I think we must get her properly assessed, first. I'm afraid it might take a few weeks before someone is available, but I'll certainly write the letter as soon as I can. This week if possible.'

'Well, thank you.'

'Thank you, Doctor.' I say, smiling. Nice man. Irish… like… I can't remember.

From the doorway I can see her. She's reading. A card. She's pretty when she smiles.

I must tell her…

Oh, the smile's gone. She's stuffing the card behind the clock. Secrets.

'Is it your birthday?'

'No, Mother. That's not till December.'

'Is it my birthday?'

'No. That's in April.'

'That's a card.'

'Yes, but it's only a note from somebody. It's not for anyone's birthday. Now, almost time for lunch. You sit there while I go and make it.'

'Is it for me?'

'No, it's for me. You're in my house this morning. You're going back to your home later. The post here is for me. Your post will be waiting for you at Bradley Drive.'

She puts a book in my hand. 'There you go. Some nice pictures to look at for a couple of minutes while I get the lunch ready. You can imagine you're wandering through all these lovely places. Look. Cornwall. Remember going there?'

Cornwall. Nice. 'Clovelly', it says. 'Olde worlde charm, steep cobbled streets.' Nice.

I can see my card. It's sticking out behind the clock. I know it's for me. She keeps hiding things. Why does she hide things?

My dear Jessica

It was sweet of you to send the card but honestly no apology was needed.

You were understandably exhausted from being phoned seven times in the night. At the best of times the dimness of the theatre and a rare opportunity to sit down and relax are conducive to sleep; you didn't stand a chance.

But far from being disappointed I have to confess that having your head on my shoulder was by far the sweetest and most exciting part of the evening. I look forward to a repeat performance!

I do worry about you though. Won't you reconsider and let me help you share your heavy responsibilities? I'd be more than willing to.

See you Friday (your mum permitting!)

Yours (truly, sincerely, faithfully and as ever)
Aaron x

'D'you fancy mushroom omel... *Mother!*'

She snatches the card out of my hand and holds it against

her chest. She's angry. I can see it. Feel it.

'How dare you read my private letters? How dare you?' She's white and trembling.

'It's not nice to snatch,' I say.

'*Not nice!*' She's making a horrible noise and banging her clenched fists against her head. 'I can't do this! I can't bear it.' She's crying.

I don't like it. I'm frightened.

'You're not content with ruining my life, but now you want to meddle in my private correspondence as well. And you blame *me* for snatching!'

I must get away.

'Oh, no you don't! You jolly well stay there in that chair and drink this juice, or I'll pour the whole bally thing over your stupid head! And see, if you spill it…'

'I want to go home.'

'You'll go home when I say so and not before, even if I have to chain you to the table! I've got things I absolutely *have* to do this morning and I am not going to spend six more hours scouring the lanes and ditches looking for you. So for goodness' sake, just drink that juice.'

'Can I go home now? I don't like it here.'

'And I don't like you being here either, so that makes two of us.'

She glares at me. I don't like it.

Oh, I've got some juice. I like juice.

'Well, hallelujah! Five minutes' peace.'

'May I have a biscuit?'

'You can have a whole tin-full of biscuits if it'll keep you quiet and out of mischief.'

Bourbons. I like bourbons.

'Thank you.'

'You're welcome.'

She stands watching me. Then she's crouching beside me. Too close. Is she going to…?

'Mum,' she whispers, 'I'm so sorry. I didn't mean to shout. I know you can't help it. But I'm so, so tired. Forgive me.'

'Can I have a biscuit?'

'Course you can.'

I must phone Eugene. Tell him. Where's the number? Ah, I know. She showed me. Press 4.

It's ringing.

'Hello?'

'Hello? Who's this?'

'It's me.'

'Mother?' the voice hisses. 'What on earth are you doing ringing at this hour? It's three o'clock in the morning over here! What's wrong?'

'Where's George?'

'Mother, is Jessica there? Put her on the phone will you? Now.'

'I need to tell Eugene. He's my son. Can I speak to Eugene, please?'

'This is Eugene speaking, Mum. I'm in Australia. And it's the middle of the night over here.'

'I have to tell you about Lionel.'

'Lionel's been dead for years. Now listen. I'm going to ring off. Your phone bills will be sky high if you keep phoning us like this. I'll ring Jessica tomorrow and sort something out so I can have a chat with you another time.'

'I need to speak to Eugene.'

'You can. But not tonight. Bye, Mother.'

It's ringing.

'Hello? Hello?' I say. Why doesn't he answer?

The policeman is calling somebody. It must be official then. Have I done something bad? Why am I here? Why isn't he taking me home?

'Hello? Mrs Burden?... Yes. This is PC Colin Armitage. I brought your mum home when she went wandering into somebody's house a couple of weeks ago... Yes, I'm afraid so... No, this time she was off to see her solicitor.' He laughs. 'Well, she is *now*! She's quite happy at the moment but we can't keep her here all night and we can't take her back to an empty house... By all means... That'll be fine. See you soon.'

He gives a big sigh. 'What are we going to do with you, Doris?'

'Is that my solicitor? Can I go now?'

'Yep. You can go soon, darling, but we can't leave you all on your ownio. Your daughter's on her way. But you need to be more careful, you know. Next time you decide to go for a wee dander it mightn't be somebody friendly like me that picks you up and then where would you be, eh?'

'Oh, you look lovely,' I say. She's all dressed up. 'Are you going somewhere nice?'

'I *was* somewhere nice,' she says. Her eyes aren't smiling.

'Have I got time to get changed before we go?'

'No, Mother, the only changing you're going to do is into your pyjamas. Thank you so much for taking care of her, PC Armitage.'

'I'm only sorry I had to spoil your evening, Mrs Burden. Like your mum says, looks like it was something special. Hope you can make up for it later on.'

'If only.'

'They're a real handful, aren't they? You need eyes in the back of your head. Can we give you a run home?'

'That's very kind, but we have a car outside, thanks.'

'OK then. Night night, Doris. Best of luck, Mrs Burden.'

She holds me too tightly. The doors swing shut behind us. It's cold out here.

A man hops out of a black car right outside the door. Smart. He's smiling.

'Mum, this is Aaron. Aaron Wiseman. He's very kindly said he'll run us home.'

'Good evening, Mrs Mannering,' he says.

I shake his hand. 'Good evening,' I say. He looks nice.

She sits in the back with me. He's the chauffeur. I wonder where we're going. Somewhere smart by the look of it. Good.

It's very quiet. Purring along.

'This is a lovely taxi. Is it yours?'

He laughs. 'Thank you. Yes, it is mine. I'm glad you like it.'

'Are you a policeman?' I ask him.

'No. I'm a friend of your daughter's. I'm a solicitor.'

Hah! I was right. I told them that.

'I was coming to see you.'

'Were you?'

'We need somewhere private.'

'Right.'

'Are you taking me somewhere nice?'

'I hope so. I'm taking you home. And it's always nice to come home when you've been away.'

'Are we going out for dinner?'

He smiles. 'Not tonight. It's too late for going out now.'

She leans right over. 'Mother. Look at me. We. Are. Going. Home. It's bedtime.'

'You look nice, dear. Are you going somewhere special?'

'No. I'm taking you home.'

Everybody's very quiet. I'm tired.

Beatrice is crying.

I don't know what to say.

'Crying won't change anything. Come on, Bea. We'll sort something out.'

'You won't tell, will you?'

'Mother. Wake up. We're home. Thank you so much, Aaron. And I'm so sorry about tonight.'

'Don't be. Glad I could help.'

The driver gets out of the car and opens the door for me. He helps me. A real gentleman.

'Thank you,' I say.

'You're welcome.' Lovely smile. I smile back.

'Thank you,' she says. 'For the dinner, and the lift. Thank you. I'm truly sorry. Goodnight.' She isn't looking at him.

'Oh.' He stands there. The smile has gone. He moves a step towards her. 'Jessica, let me at least stay until you're ready, and run you home.'

She shakes her head without looking up. 'Please.'

'I can wait in the car.'

Her fingers are clenched on my elbow. She shakes her head. 'We'll be fine. I can't go home now. I'll have to stay here tonight.'

'Fair enough, but well, what about a coffee? Compensate for missing dessert.'

'I'm so sorry. I feel really bad about that. After all the trouble you went to.'

'Trouble? I don't think so.' He's looking at her in a funny way. 'But it would be a shame if the evening ended sooner than it needed to, don't you think?'

'I should feel even more guilty if we ruined what's left of it for you.'

'Oh, I wouldn't call having coffee with you a ruined evening.' His voice is all chocolatey.

'But you might if... No. Besides, I do need to concentrate on Mother. She's always slow to settle after wandering.'

'Well, if you're sure.'

'Thank you very much,' I say. 'Are you a policeman?'

'No, I'm not.'

'I'm sorry,' she whispers.

'So am I,' he says.

I turn at the door. He's still standing there. Watching. He looks very smart.

'Are we going somewhere special?'

She hustles me inside and shuts the door. Why is she crying? I don't like it when she's sad.

Chapter 18
Eight years earlier

SOME DAYS IT feels like going into a tunnel. I need to hold onto me so I don't get lost. I wish Mamma was here. I don't like the dark. She knows that.

Jessica doesn't understand. She thinks everything is the same. She doesn't know about all the things that're going missing. I don't tell her. I can't worry about her too. I'm too busy hanging on. She's so good to me.

But she mustn't know about the papers. I mustn't tell her. I mustn't tell her. I mustn't tell her.

The only thing is, I don't know where they are. I can't find them. They're in a safe place, but where it is? I must find them. I must.

I need George.

The den is such a mess. Why do boys have to be so untidy? Books, papers, boxes everywhere.

Where to start? Think, Doris, think. Where would you put them?

In the desk? I always hated the desk. It's too big for this room. And it looks so raggy with everything showing. I like drawers. Everything hidden away. I'll tidy these away first.

Goodness. So many books. Jessica can have them; she's always loved reading. Ah, her favourites – Thomas Hardy, Geoffrey Farnoll, Jane Austen. Is this one hers? Lewis Grassic

Gibbon? I don't remember. Yes – *Jessica M. Mannering* – such neat writing.

What did I come in here for? I can't remember.

She could have warned me. Nobody tells me anything nowadays.

'We're going down to the surgery this morning, Mum. Nothing to worry about. They like to keep an eye on their older patients.'

'Does Beatrice know?'

'Beatrice?'

'Yes.'

'Beatrice is in London. She'll be at work right now but you could ring her and tell her tonight.'

'Who's looking after the children?'

'Beatrice hasn't got any children.'

'Yes, she has. One of each.'

'No, that's not Beatrice, that's Pandora, your granddaughter, who's got the children.'

'That's what I said.'

'Oh, sorry. I misunderstood.'

The doctor's very young. And too thin. He needs some of my raspberry trifle.

'Hello, Mrs Mannering. My name's Dr Noble. Your daughter tells me you haven't been yourself lately.'

'Does she? Well, that must be right, but I feel fine now.'

'So what's been wrong?'

'Nothing. I'm fine.'

I look at him more closely. He *is* looking thin. I don't think he's very well.

'Would you excuse me for a moment?'

It's quiet in here after he's gone. I read the notices. *Have you had your winter flu injection? The Meningitis Trust: Signs and Symptoms…* Why do they put up so many posters? You can't read them all. There isn't time. *Obesity kills.*

The voice is low but it carries in the silence: '...why you brought her to see us today?'

You'd think they'd close the door. It's confidential. I wouldn't want other people hearing about *me*.

'It's lots of little things really. Sometimes she forgets people are dead – her parents, her husband, her brother. People that have been dead for years.' Sounds like... but I know it can't be. It happens nowadays. Voices... things not right...

'Right.'

'And some days it's like she's forgotten how to do things that were second nature to her before; cooking, crosswords, gardening, reading, knitting.'

'Could you give me a concrete example maybe?'

'Well, the other day she was going to make drop scones. You know, the kind you make on a griddle. They were one of her specialities. Only she didn't seem to know she had to beat the eggs...'

I do that sometimes.

'...but she still surprises me with what she *can* do. Last week my son found her connecting the TV to the video with a new scart-to-scart, and neither of *us* bought it, so she must have. I mean, how can she be so vague one minute and understand something as technical as that the next? It doesn't make sense.'

'Well, it's quite common for older people to forget things – names, places. And get more clumsy.'

I could have told her *that*!

'Well, it seems like more than that.'

'Has she taken any different medication recently? Sometimes people react to certain drugs.'

Ah. I *knew* there was...

'Not that I'm aware of, but then I don't know everything she does. I'm not there all the time.'

'Well, there's nothing in her notes to suggest... as you know, her own doctor is on leave this week, but I'll have a chat with him when he gets back. He may be able to throw some light on this.'

'She gets very frustrated when I don't understand – when she uses the wrong word, or name, or something.'

'Mm.'

'But then she can be fine when visitors call.'

'Right. Well, thank you. That's helpful. Would you like to come in too while I chat to your mum?'

The doctor comes back in. He's been ages. Jessica's with him. Why is she here? She doesn't look directly at me. I want to tell her... but he's asking me questions. Funny questions. What year is it? Who's the prime minister? Think of an object... Makes you want to say something silly.

'That's fine, Mrs Mannering. We'll keep an eye on you for a bit. See how you go.'

'Thank you.'

'Are you saying there's nothing...?'

Jessica is blinking fast. Why?

'I don't know. But don't worry, your mother's entire future care won't hinge on one assessment! I expect her own doctor will want to monitor her. I'll leave a note.'

'I started her on folic acid supplements. It said they enhance cognitive function, particularly the memory.'

'Right. You could have a chat with Dr Robartz about that.'

She's quiet all the way home. I keep my eyes shut. I don't want to see the look on her face.

She said I could ring her. Hash 2. Easy.

'Beatrice?'

'Speaking.'

'Hello. It's me. Jessica said I could ring you.'

'Good grief. Do you need permission to ring your own sister these days?'

'I went to the doctor.'

'Did you? Something wrong? Is it something serious?'

'I don't want to talk about it.'

'Why did you ring me, then?'

'Don't you want to know?'

'For goodness' sake, Doris. Are you dying? Is that it? Should I speak to Jessica?'

'You mustn't.'

'So why did you ring, then?'

'The doctor said so.'

'The doctor said you should ring me?'

'No. Don't be silly. I wanted you to know… I have to tell her.'

'Tell who?'

'Jessica.'

I hear her suck in her breath. 'Tell… *Jessica*? No! No, you mustn't, Doris. You promised. Remember?'

'Did I? I don't remember. But the doctor said…'

'Doris, listen to me. This is important. You mustn't tell her. And you mustn't let her see the papers. Have you got them somewhere safe?'

'What?'

'The papers. You *know!* Have you?'

'Yes.'

'Where?'

'Never you mind.'

'I do mind. With you forgetting things, who knows where anything is?'

'You never cared a diddlysquat before.'

'That's not true.'

'I'm tired. Thank you for calling. Bye.'

'No, Doris! Hold on. Let me speak to Jessica. Is she there?'

'No. She doesn't live here any more.'

'Well, I know *that*! But she's often at your house. Oh, never mind. I'll ring her myself.'

She makes everything so confusing. But then she always did.

It's the same today. I feel sad. No reason. I just do.

I know it's sad that George has gone. Lionel. Reuben. And Jessica is sad sometimes. I see it. But, I don't know. It isn't that kind of sad.

I must get on. The den is such a mess. I wish George was

here to keep it all straight. He knows where things are. I'll start tidying it up and then perhaps I'll come across those papers when I'm not really looking.

This sadness. It's not official. It's just informal.

Jessica's finished putting my washing on the line. I can do that. I did it this morning. I don't know why she has to do it again.

'Jessica,' I say.

'Yes?'

'Am I going loopy?'

She looks at me like she thinks I'm going to ask her something difficult. 'Why ever would you think that?'

'Only, I can't find my purse. I know I had it yesterday.'

'And there it is on the table. I expect you popped it down when you thought of something else to do.'

'I do forget things sometimes.'

'So do I and I'm 20 years younger, so don't fret yourself about that!'

She drags out the hoover and starts on the sitting room. I can do it; I told her that. But I know she likes helping people.

I watch her. She's so efficient, so thorough. So *busy*.

Jessica is very conscientious. She works hard and is always polite and helpful in class. A credit to her parents and the school, that's what they said.

She probably doesn't have time to notice. I hope I'm gone before she sees it. I don't want her doing more for me. She's got her own home to run, her own family. And I can manage. It doesn't matter if I can't remember everything. Some things are best forgotten.

She's a smart girl, Pandora. A bit starved looking, but she oozes confidence. I watch her now curled up on my settee, arms wrapped about her model's legs. She seems lit up.

'What d'you think, Gran? Italy, here I come! Dreamy or what?'

'Sounds amazing. What does your mother think?'

'She says it's my life. I have to decide what's important.'

'What about... what was his name? Eddie, was it? Eric?'

She tosses one hand. 'Oh *him*. Edwin. That finished *ages* ago.' A couple of months ago she was turning a foil strip around her ring finger with a faraway smile on her lips.

'And it's for – two years, did you say?'

'Two years initially. But I'll be home for holidays. And I'll phone you, often. Promise.'

'Until some Italian heart-throb sweeps you off in a gondola!'

'That's *Venice*! I'm going to be in *Florence*. *Fab* place, Gran. Like a life-sized museum. Totally ancient statues, bridges, buildings... you'll have to come and visit, and I'll take you round and show you *everything*.'

'And the job? Is it what you really want?'

'What's not to like about a walloping pay-rise, and loads of travel, and a personal expense account, and my own car? I tell you, it's a million light years away from what the Newcastle office gave me.'

'I hope it'll be everything you dream of, dear.'

'*Will* you come and see me?'

'I expect you'll be terribly busy soaking up all the culture and the sunshine, and falling in love with dark-eyed Italians who'll serenade you with cornettos.' She laughs. 'And you'll come back looking like a fashion plate.'

'The Italians *do* know how to dress, don't they? Gorgeous clothes, shoes, handbags, jewellery. I can't wait.'

'That'll suit you to a T, Pandora.'

'Even the *old* ladies look like a million dollars over there.'

'Well, the ones you see out and about in the tourist attractions, maybe. But I imagine some of them slop about at home sometimes, don't they? The ones who feed 30 peasants at harvest time on Dolmio products and sun-ripened peaches!'

'Well, *I* think it's a sign of a civilised culture when old folk respect themselves enough to buy nice clothes and pamper themselves.'

'I'm only teasing you, Pandy.'

'Did you see that thing on the news about old people in *this* country – Monday, I think it was? Saying they ought to be allowed to die if they feel they're a burden on their families.'

'I did, yes.'

'Well, I bet the Italian oldies wouldn't feel they *were* a burden.'

'Maybe. Depends on the family, I think.'

'Well, you'll never be a burden in *our* family, Gran.'

'I hope not, sweetheart, I do hope not. But thank you for saying so.'

The back door clicks.

'Only me.' Jessica is looking particularly smart for a shopping expedition. Italy must be having an impact already.

Pandora bounces to her feet. 'Hi, Mum. I've been telling Gran all about Florence and the job and everything. She absolutely *has* to come out and visit while I'm there.'

'Because in Italy old people aren't a burden on their families,' I add.

'Goodness, where did that come from?' Jessica says.

'Well, you *know*,' Pandora explains, before I can elaborate. 'Over there they're into family, aren't they? The old folk go on living with them, cooking, keeping house, all that sort of thing. But here, they don't have any kind of *role*, do they? They sort of go to waste.'

'So it stands to reason they ought to simply shuffle off and free up the space for the next generation to live graciously,' I say with a smile at my earnest granddaughter.

'Mum! Don't encourage her.'

'No, but they said on that programme – sometimes they *want* to go. They don't want to be a burden.'

'Well, I don't know who "they" were,' Jessica says, 'but I do know it would be absolutely wrong to take a life for such a selfish reason.'

'But surely that would be being *un*selfish,' Pandora protests.

Jessica interrupts sharply. 'If anybody's thinking they're a burden then it's up to the family and the doctors and everybody to make sure they *do* feel loved and wanted and valuable.'

'Like apparently they all do in Italy, Jessica,' I chip in, willing her to lighten up. Why does she sound so cross?

Nobody seems to have heard me.

'But old folk *are* a burden on society, Mum,' Pandora says. 'The number of oldies is rising, what with the baby boom and everything. We can't *keep* stumping up for more and more folk who aren't contributing anything to the economy or to society. Everybody else will suffer.'

'I'm shocked.' Jessica looks at her daughter as if she's brought something nasty into the room on her shoe. 'I really am shocked. I thought you'd have more respect for old people, for *life*, than that.'

I open my mouth to say something soothing but Pandora chimes in before I can speak. 'No, but you have to be sensible about these things. Gran can see it. *She* knows what I'm talking about. She doesn't want to be a burden. Not that she would be, of course. But she wouldn't *want* to be either, would you, Gran?'

'No, dear. But that's hardly a virtue. I don't think *anybody* wants to be a burden.'

'Well, all I can say is, heaven help us all if we dare to grow old and senile!' Jessica says caustically.

'You'd better emigrate to Italy!' I say.

She hunches her jacket closer around her shoulders. 'We must go, Pandora, if you're going to fit in everything you have on that list for today.'

'It's the big shop, Gran. Designer labels all the way. Got to look the part.'

'I'm going along merely to carry the bags,' Jessica says with a grin. 'Trying to make sure I'm still of *some* use in our family.'

I am suddenly enveloped in young arms and expensive perfume. 'I'll come and show you my new wardrobe before I go. Promise. Love you.'

I just feel sad.

Chapter 19
Eleven years earlier

THE CHRISTMAS TABLE looks fantastic, more festive even than usual. I've kept to red and gold this time. It's almost superstitious, this compulsion to vary it every year. I have to make it bright and welcoming in a big way this time – we need all the help we can get. For the children especially, but for each other too.

Strange, really, I decided last year it would be black and silver this time and I bought some decorations half-price in January in those colours. But black feels wrong, this first Christmas without Lionel.

Lionel. Even thinking about him makes my knees cave in. How can he *not* be here? Or anywhere. I'd settle for anywhere.

Thirty-two. That's all he was. The same age as I was when I conceived him; our mistake. It's another unseen but painful Christmas memory. The mulled wine the children left out for Santa seemed to have gone to George's head; he was as frisky as the proverbial reindeer. If he *had* to wait up till midnight he had 'something much more exciting' in mind than peeling sprouts... caution was for ordinary mundane nights not Christmas Eve. I was relieved we made it to the bedroom – the youngsters were wont to appear unexpectedly looking for a sneak preview of the treats in store... not their parents *in flagrante*!

The isolation of those memories remains with me. To the

children Dad has been dead 16 years. Old news. The sting has long gone. And to them we've always been old. They can have no concept of him as the eager lover. Or of my yearning in that empty bed.

But the impact of *Lionel's* death is different. Everyone feels that. Intensely. I know they do. Which is why I'm pulling out all the stops this year. Dear, dear Lionel, who was as much loved and wanted as all the others as soon as he arrived. So much more like his father in appearance than any of his siblings, but with none of George's gentle acceptance of the humdrum. My youngest was a magnet for danger.

It was Lionel who wandered off exploring rock pools as the tide came in while my attention was on shielding the girls' modesty behind the beach towels. Lionel who set the chemistry lab on fire when he tinkered with the bunsen burners. Lionel who took off into the rainforests of Tasmania and was out of communication for three whole months.

What would life have held for him had he lived, I wonder? A roving diplomat negotiating peace-deals? Bringing aid to refugees? Conquering some remote mountain? Who knows? I'm glad George was spared this worst of all losses.

It was painful to write the place-names in gold on red cards this year. I hate these first times. Our first Christmas without '*Lionel*'. But everyone made a supreme effort to bridge the gap, to be there for one another. All except Eugene, of course; nobody expects him to travel halfway round the world just for a family get-together.

There they all are – round my table.

'*James*'. Right next to me because he'll be the first to leap up to help – even now, in his teens, when most boys shun any evidence of sentiment or sensitivity. His sweet nature is as unselfconscious today as when he could barely reach to put dishes on the table. Dear James. And he's so good for Jessica.

'*Jessica*'. What would I have done without her during this horrible year? What would I have done without her full stop?

'*Lewis*'. He'll shadow her silently but without complaint and

I guess we have to be satisfied with that. I feel guilty, disloyal even, wishing in my heart that she'd found someone with more drive, more suited to her. I fear she's had a hard struggle to drag this strange man towards her ambitions for their family. She's never spoken of it but where is the spark? Where is the affinity?

'*Pandora*'. Much as I adore my eldest granddaughter, I want her out of my line of vision at the meal-table. I can't bear to see good food wasted.

'*Adeline*'. She 'might be bringing a friend' this year. A male friend. I've left a space and a card to be filled in once I know his name and if he lasts that long. I can only hope he's more suitable than either of her husbands. Ah dear. She was never an easy child, and she's certainly not a comfortable adult. But I must take some responsibility. I'm her mother, I brought her up. If only something of Jessica's thoughtfulness had rubbed off on her. But then maybe our eldest was an impossible act to follow.

'*Sydney*'. '*Gwen*'. '*Derek*'. '*Barbara*'. The light glints off their scrolling names. I'm touched to have my brothers coming with their wives this year, a show of solidarity I didn't expect. But even this bonus is tinged with sadness because Reuben's not here. It's at times like this the losses all crowd in and threaten to stifle me. My eldest brother, my husband, and now my youngest son, all taken though illness. Accidents or wars would seem more modern and forgivable.

'*Beatrice*'. She always comes for Christmas. I couldn't deny her that, especially given the circumstances. But still my heart sinks. I think she's the reason I find Adeline so difficult to be with sometimes – all dimples and charm when the world smiles on her, all petulance and temper when she's thwarted. Aunt and niece. Both twice divorced, both materially rich, both coming for Christmas. Can genes leap sideways like that? It's double-edged.

I shall be glad when this charade is over and we can settle back into mourning.

Chapter 20
Eleven years earlier

I AM A GRANDMOTHER. A *grand*mother!

Her name is Pandora Marguerite. Six pounds three ounces of fragrant, beautiful babyness. I can't believe the feelings she induces in me.

I want to tell the world about this miracle.

Dear Eugene and Jane

I'm sure you're agog to know all about your new little niece. From someone impartial! I am bursting with pride! Well, she's perfect. Like a miniature Jessica. And Jess is such a natural with her...

My mind follows this letter to the other side of the world. It still feels strange, having a child of mine so far away, surrounded by people I scarcely know.

I turn my back on the garden and move into the house, leaving the melancholy thoughts to shrivel in the warmth of the conservatory. This is a time for celebration. I am a *grandmother*!

The emptiness is palpable. They've all gone. Before, there was always someone here to fill the gaps left by those departing the nest. Now there's only me. And there are yawning holes in my role too. I wander through these rooms that have witnessed all the phases of family life over the past 30 years. The unnatural quiet seems to seep into my bones. I feel hollowed out. My heart cries out for the clutter and disarray, even for the assumption that I would clear up behind them.

My bedroom. I sink down onto the bed I shared with George for all those years – I can't bear to replace it. Grief, regret and longing jostle together. I miss his touch, his smile, his love, every single day.

When the children departed, I could rejoice in spite of the sadness. They were going out to challenge the world. It was part of my job description to make them independent and I'd fulfilled that role. George's departure – never to return – is unalloyed sorrow. There is no solace. No straw to save me from drowning.

And how I regret... Long before I knew anything about the science of inherent gender differences and personality traits, I resented his habits. Routinely leaving his chair pulled out from the table, his still-buttoned shirt inside his jumper, suds in the shower. I rectified these offences, day after day after day. I *had* to. But I did it with a bad grace. Often. Now I would trade every orderly room for one sock left lying on the bathroom floor, one stack of half-read newspapers on the table, the feel of his arm around me, holding me back from a pressing task, one more time.

I leave the room abruptly.

Jessica's room. Her presence pervades it even now. I can see her yet perched on the window seat, lost in a book, her finger absently twirling a curl. I glimpse her turning her face this way and that in the mirror looking for... what? Imperfections? Resemblances?

When she first left home, I missed her more than she will ever know. I was totally bereft. Perhaps that was inevitable. She was the first to fly the nest and I had no experience to prepare me for the sense of desolation. But now, looking back, I suspect it was more than inexperience. With her departure went the peacemaker, the exemplar, the glue of our family. Exactly how she manages to be so essential to us all is a mystery I've often pondered. She's unique.

But I do know that she occupies a special place in my affections, which makes me at once guilty and glad. Guilt is synonymous with parenting, of course, but in the secret places of my heart I know that in Jessica's case this is something more. I chose her. She wasn't the natural product of our love. No, we made a conscious decision to bring her into our family. Have I been over-compensating, subconsciously justifying my own actions? Has my love for Adeline, Eugene and Lionel been diminished because of her specialness?

Not that she demands such devotion. No, it's her selflessness that inspires it. But it hasn't been all good. I fear it was her kind nature that led her to marry Lewis. He's inoffensive, but he's no match for her in intellect, wit or zest for life. I want to wind him up. But how can a parent influence something as complex as the choice of a spouse? That's what growing up means: making your own decisions and living with the consequences.

'Give over, Doris,' George protested once. 'The lad's fine. And I've never heard her complain, so don't you go putting ideas into her head.'

It's not my style to say anything after the event anyway. And now she has Pandora Marguerite, and Lewis is as proud as any father I know.

Adeline's room. There's little of Adeline the child, the teenager, left in here. She insisted on it being modernised when it became her occasional and adult base – 'adult' meaning a lockable door, a double bed.

The worry when this second daughter left home was of a different order from the first. Where would her rebellious nature lead her? But in spite of the anxiety, I felt relief. Tension left with her. George and I could relax, the boys could romp and tease without fear of the consequences.

Since then she's seldom returned alone and, sad to admit, she's always better diluted. At first it was university 'friends' for whom Bradley Drive became a convenient place to spend whatever hours were left for sleep. And then there was Percy…

She was 22.

'His name's Percival Quentin Bartholomew and he is *so* well off.' Deep sigh, rapt expression. 'His family's something to do with tarmac. And I have to say, his ma and pa are lovely. You'll like them. And you'll absolutely *love* their house. I can't remember how many rooms, but I got lost every single day.'

We lived in daily expectation of hearing that Percival Quentin had beaten a hasty retreat long before we were invited to inspect the said mansion but no, something in our daughter seemed to appeal to him. She paraded down the aisle, wearing antique lace and a genuine diamond tiara, to become the wife of the heir to a fortune. For three years and nine months she has adorned his arm and frittered his money, turning a blind eye to his recreational pursuits, so his sudden decision to end the farce has taken her by storm. Even now, it's Jessica who's bearing the brunt of her outrage, not me. Thank God there are no children to suffer through the humiliation of these divorce proceedings.

'Well, there wouldn't be, would there?' Adeline spat out. 'He's into *men*!'

It grieves me to see her emerging so embittered by the experience.

'Men! I've finished with the lot of them.' Exactly what 'finished' means to Adeline is unclear to me. She rang yesterday to say she's bringing someone called Ferdie this weekend. And will I please 'be nice to him'. 'He'll sleep in my room. So please don't go all prudish on me. Remember, I'm still hurting over Percy.' 'Hurting' too comes from a different dictionary.

She has outgrown not only her place within the family home, but our moral code and our values. A hard fact for a mother.

The boys' room – as I call it, in spite of the partition. Spartan. Essentially male. It's become something of a dumping ground of late, but in my mind it's littered with discarded clothes, Lego models, weird circuit-boards, balls of various shapes and sizes.

By the time Eugene went away I knew what emotions to anticipate, but I was unprepared for the sheer *size* of his absence. We'd grown so used to his exuberance that we scarcely noticed the racket he created, and it was not until the house deflated without him that I started to understand his contribution to the life of our family.

And his going taught me something else. Having a stretch of water between me and my children unsettled me far more than having them distant, but on the same island. It was irrational given the ease with which the Navy could have returned him to me in an emergency. But he was only 17.

Eugene was never a good communicator and his letters home soon dwindled to the occasional postcard and birthday cards. Or important news.

'*Met a fab lass in Melbourne. Jane. Going to stay there for a month in December. Have a happy Christmas. Think of me roasting on the beach with this gorgeous chick while you try to stay warm beside the fire with turkey. Ha Ha!*' was vintage Eugene.

Jane has changed him. He left the Navy when they got married last year. He now has a mortgage, and their first child is due later in December. No, not their first... that was a stillbirth, born prematurely two years ago. 'We just said to folk they didn't tell us what sex it was, Mum. Truth is, the doctors couldn't tell. Weird, huh? Makes you feel, I don't know... knowing you made... that.' Only the darkness of their verandah enabled him to tell me then. It was good though, sharing that moment, being the Mum he needed again. And going to Australia, seeing a foreign country, my eldest boy getting married, maturing. Precious memories.

But tinged with sadness now. It came at a price.

'We have to go to see them, George. You can't expect them

to travel, not this distance. And definitely not once they've got children. Besides, we don't *need* so much land, do we?'

'It's yours. It's up to you if you want to sell it. And it's your money.' His lips tight. Hurting.

'They're family. Don't you *want* to see them? Watch your grandchildren growing up?'

'He chose to go over there.'

Buying the house, selling the land – the two conflicts he and I never resolved. And now it's too late.

But it's Lionel whose going has opened up this hole I'm floundering in today. My baby. The last to leave home.

Losing his dad at a tender age – only 16 – had a profound effect on him. 'If I'm going to peg it that young, I need to get on and live now, Mum. There's a big old world out there.'

Lionel wants to 'find' himself and no doubt he's perfectly capable of fending for himself. But all the logic in the world doesn't make it any easier to have him out there, I know not where, discovering his potential – especially as his letter-writing makes Eugene look like Boswell.

I wonder sometimes, is it hardest for the youngest? Do they have more to prove? In Lionel's case, being six years younger than Eugene, he had several years to experience the life of an only child with ageing parents – even a dead parent. He's seen both his sisters and his brother establish themselves in good jobs, get married – well, Adeline *was* settled – start families. No wonder he needs to get away, spread his clipped wings.

What will life hold for him? I pray daily, *Keep him safe*, but is anybody out there listening? These worries seem so much heavier without George to share them. What a debt I owe this man who stood behind me and beside me through 27 years of marriage. Happy years. I wish I could feel as secure about my children's choices.

But I must shake off these gloomy thoughts.

Pandora – my baby granddaughter – I have to keep saying it – my *grand*daughter! – is coming here this Saturday. Her first visit to Bradley Drive. I want her life to be full of happiness and love. No regrets. No guilt.

This is a new beginning.

How George would have revelled in another little girl to love. Especially Jessica's.

Chapter 21
Twelve years earlier

I WATCH FROM the bedroom window seeing, but unseen by my family. The tears are salty still on my face.

It's so rare for George to be cross that his words repeat through my head. 'A man's got his pride, Doris. You can't expect me to *like* it.'

If he's dwelling on our argument at all there's no sign of it. He's romping through the garden roped to four children. Periodically he glances back to check on them but mostly he stampedes as one of them. And everywhere I see the evidence of his concessions. The tree-house he built so painstakingly, a firm favourite with all four. The summerhouse saved from ruin several times by his timely roof repairs, simply to preserve the magic of '*The secret abode of Mr Tawny Owl and his friends*', the enchanted creatures the children grew up with in my bedtime stories. The wigwam constructed by him out of hessian sacks and stripped willow, still standing in the grotto, half hidden by the holly bush he raids annually for our Christmas wreath. And it's thanks to his strength that the wildest areas of this garden have been reclaimed and transformed.

'Faster! Faster!' The shrieks drag my mind back to the present.

With the end of the rope tied around her waist, Jessica has forgotten teenage dignity and is squealing with the rest.

What a beautiful child. And how good she is with her younger brothers and sister. All her life I've watched her anxiously, but so far at least there's been no evidence of the moods and sulks I dreaded. Will they come later? George says not: she's simply 'a thoroughly decent lassie'. But then, she is the apple of his eye; always has been. An inexplicable affinity.

The human caterpillar squirms around the twin junipers we planted when Adeline was born. And now here she is, a pretty little thing, with her fair curls and wide blue eyes, clutching her father's jacket, darting backward glances at her brother, whose feet pound dangerously close to her white socks. This morning's hysterics are forgotten. But not by me. It was a wake-up call that made me realise how spoilt she is. How she trades on George's easy-going nature. How the other children give in to her to avoid a scene, and I too, ambitious though I am for my offspring's characters, collude at times, to deflect a tantrum. Petulance can cast an ugly shadow even on the loveliest features. Would she have been the selfish creature she is if I hadn't compensated for the things I did before she was ever born? I must redouble my efforts to rectify the damage while she's still impressionable.

Whoops, there goes Lionel. Head-over-heels into the grass, sending the whole line of them flying. I can hear their laughter from here. Well, the boys' anyway. Adeline is wailing, but... ah, George has it all under control. They're up again. And they're off, Adeline now in front, protected by her father.

How much more straightforward the boys are. No wiles. No subtlety. Their aggression flashes openly at times, but they don't seem capable of subterfuge. I love the way they accept me, as I am, my discipline alongside my standards. And I know I've been a less obsessive mother with them from the outset. You worry so with the first. By the time you get to the third, well, everything's diluted.

I smile now watching Eugene, tall and gangling as his hormones surge into action, propelling Lionel forwards with a guiding hand on his shoulder, and I suspect secretly willing the little one to trip again and send them all flying.

This is exactly what I always dreamed of: my own family, happy, secure, loved and loving. A home close to the countryside with a large garden and instant playmates. How fortunate we are, George and I.

I watch all five charge like a Chinese dragon into the trees at the foot of the garden and vanish from sight.

Only then do I turn away and let my gaze wander over this house that has been such a bone of contention in my marriage. I love every stone and tile of it. I love its moods, its ability to evolve to accommodate the growth spurts of our family. I love its spaciousness and its graciousness. I love the fact that it's our exclusive territory... at least it is in *my* perceptions.

I have no idea why my grandmother May left me such a handsome bequest. If she knew, Mamma refused to be drawn on the subject. For George it has always been mine, never his. He has old-fashioned ideas about his responsibilities as head of the house, and they do not include a monetary contribution from his wife, never mind the larger share. And even with the promotion to manager at the textile mill, his salary couldn't buy or maintain this property.

His stubbornness still rankles. 'Look, the money's yours. You can do what you like with it. But I want to support my family on *my* money. That's my job.'

'And you do. But Grandmamma's bequest is too much simply to bank. It would be much more sensible to invest it. You said so yourself, remember? It would buy us a nice family home, somewhere for the children to play. We can choose it together. It's your money too.'

'No. It isn't.'

He remained immovable, refusing even to look for a house. When I eventually found Bradley Drive he came to view it but shrugged his shoulders and said dismissively, 'If it's what you want. It's your money.'

Today's dispute, 14 years on, was about adding a conservatory. It's something I've always wanted. 'It would mean we could enjoy the garden for longer each year.' Surely a trump card given the energy we've both put into creating this fabulous garden. But no. George makes up a few specious reservations but nobody's fooled. It's so frustrating! He's happy to have me using his money all the years I've been at home bringing up the children, but he can't accept mine. Men!

What a curious thing marriage is. I used to wonder about Mamma and Father. They were adults; they'd chosen each other... against all advice. Why didn't they talk about their differences and agree a solution, calmly, rationally? Why did we children have to endure the weeks of tension, the silences, until the caress, the kiss that signalled the end of hostilities? Was it because she'd 'married beneath her', like Aunt Hester said? Was the gulf too big to leap?

Experience has taught me why. Living together is so much more complicated than my childish notions of happily-ever-after. As husbands go, George has to be one of the most accommodating, honourable and trustworthy, but even he has his limits. Irrational sometimes, at least in my eyes. Using my money is one of them.

Speaking of limits, my sister, Beatrice, comes tomorrow. And there's nothing irrational about George's dread of her visits. I share it. We huddle in our bed at night and dissect her words and actions, anticipate her next move, and sigh with relief when she leaves again. Secretly we acknowledge the debt we owe her; together we scheme to reduce any influence she may have on our growing family.

She was always the odd one out. To my brothers I was one of the gang, a tomboy who could hold her own. Bea was always girly, looking for admiration and concessions. Even Reuben, who was mature enough to ally himself with me when the younger boys ventured into thoughtless cruelty, would on occasion join them in mocking her.

Perhaps that was why she seemed impervious to the horror of having all the boys away at the front at the same time. Mamma and I lived in daily expectation of that dreaded telegram. Every soldier who limped down the street or tapped his way along the railings, every house that remained shuttered after the news arrived, reminded me of the real danger the boys faced. Bea just lived for the time she could clock off from the munitions factory and go to dance the night away.

How different the lives of my children, Jessica, Eugene, Adeline and Lionel, who have no memories of the deprivations or the fear.

But are they any happier? I shall always worry.

Chapter 22
Fifteen years earlier

I FLING AN ARM around my sister's shoulders.

'What is it, Bea? Tell me. Come on. Tell me what's upset you.'

'I am so... Oh, Doris, what am I going to *do*?' she wails.

'About what? Come on. You'll feel better if you share it.'

She was always given to the melodramatic so I'm completely unprepared for what comes next.

'I'm pregnant.'

I'm stunned into silence.

The paroxysms redouble. 'See, I knew you'd be cross.'

'Cross? Never mind that. Bea, how far on are you?'

'Three months gone.'

'And what does Mamma say?'

'I haven't told her. I haven't told anyone else. Oh Doris, I can't!' She twists her hands into knots. 'I can't tell her. What will she think of me?'

'It's a bit late for that! How on earth did this happen?'

'I thought you'd at least know *that*!' she flashes. 'Now you're married. Or are you too pure to have George poking his thing up you?'

I flush, stung not only by her crudity but the memory of my own naïvety on our wedding night, George's astonishment, his gentleness. For Mamma left that particular piece of information out of my curriculum entirely.

'But you're *not* married!' I retort, the edge of my voice sharper than I intended.

'And nice girls don't do it,' she singsongs, sarcasm in her sneer as well as her tone.

'Well... no.' It sounds lame even to me.

'Well... this one did. Get real, Jess. There's a war on. Tomorrow may be too late.'

'So are you going to get married?'

'*Married*! Good heavens, *no*! I *can't*! I'm only 16. I've got my whole life ahead of me. I can't tie myself to a baby!'

'So what *are* you going to do?'

'I don't know. That's why I came to see you. What can I do?'

I can think of nothing whatever to say so I stall for time.

'Who's the father?'

'I'm not sure.' This time she does have the grace to look embarrassed.

'For goodness' sake, Beatrice. What on earth were you thinking about?'

'It was just a bit of fun. I never dreamt...'

'Well, I can't think straight right this minute but leave it with me. I'll help you if I can. You'll need to give me time to think of something. And you're going to have to find a way to tell Mamma. You'll soon start to show.'

'I know,' she wails, fresh tears sparkling on her lashes. Not for the first time, I marvel at how pretty she is. I'd be all blotches and puffiness; she simply goes into soft focus.

I'm still lost in her problem when George comes home from work. His right leg, damaged in a childhood accident, has spared him active service, but he's on fire watch duty tonight so I have limited time to talk about today's crisis. And I have to tell him today. Tomorrow might be too late. I'm not superstitious but we agreed: because there's a war on, don't leave things till the morning, in case.

I go through the motions of listening to his day and feeding him, but once he's settled in his chair beside the fire I broach the subject.

'George, can I talk to you about something? Something serious.'

'Course you can,' he says, laying down his paper.

Several false starts later he gets up and comes across to me, dropping on one knee beside my chair.

I giggle nervously. 'Looks like you're going to propose all over again.'

'Will do if you like,' his voice gruff, 'if it'll put a smile back on your face.'

'It's Beatrice.' There, it's out now.

'What's she been up to this time?' he sighs, leaning back on his heels.

'She's pregnant.'

His smile vanishes. 'Blimey Charlie!'

'George, I'm so, so sorry. I never knew.'

'Why d'you need to apologise? It's no fault of yours.'

'But she's my sister.'

'And so you'll bear the shame. Not with me you won't, lass. That sister of yours, she's a wild card and no mistake. Everybody round here knows she's not like you. People talk. Well, never mind about that. But you're different so don't you go mixing her up with you.'

'Thank you, George. Thank you. I couldn't bear to have you think ill of me.'

'Well, I don't. And I never will. So don't you ever imagine it. You're far too good for the likes of me and I'll never know what you saw in me to make you take me on. But I thank God every night you did.'

He suddenly kisses me so thoroughly that I'm in danger of forgetting what we were talking about.

'She hasn't told anyone else yet. She thinks I can help her decide what to do. But what do I know?'

'So is the fellow going to make an honest woman out of her?'

'She says not. She says she can't tie herself down at her age.'

His eyes dilate. 'She's going to get rid of it?'

'I don't know. I didn't ask that. I didn't know *what* to say. I was so shocked.'

'But you know that's against the law. You do know *that*, don't you? And it's dangerous.'

I nod. Fear sneaks in alongside the shock.

'Better to put it up for adoption than *that*.'

'They say it's awfully hard on girls, doing that,' I venture.

'She should've thought about that before she hanky-pankied around.'

A thought hits me with the force of a hammer blow. I lean forward and clutch his hand in both mine. 'George... d'you think... could *we* adopt it?'

'*What?*'

My mind is racing with possibilities.

'Blimey! A baby! I don't know, Doris. That's a big thing to ask. And we've only just got married. I thought, well, you know, we'd have kids of our own.'

'We will. We can. Later. And the baby wouldn't be here till we'd been married nearly a year. It wouldn't look strange. Nobody needs to know it isn't ours.'

'You mean pass it off as *ours*?'

'Then people needn't know about Bea.'

George shakes his head, a strange expression on his face. 'Doris, lass, you're something else, you know that?'

'Is that good?'

'You've no business to be that unselfish. Beats me how you and Beatrice came out of the same family.'

'So, would you?'

'I'll think about it. And that's all I'm saying on the subject tonight. But I'll say this for you, Doris Mannering, I reckon I didn't know the half of it the day I married you.'

'I'm glad you did though,' I say, meaning it. 'I like being married to you.'

He laughs and pulls me close. 'Well, I'm pleased to hear that because I'm quite partial to you too.'

It's a raw November day in Inverness when Beatrice goes into labour. At last. She must be nearly two weeks late by my reckoning.

Condensation runs down the windows of the room she and I have been renting for four months now. The lino on the floor chills our chilblains. The fire splutters spasmodically, but any heat it emits is instantly absorbed by the drying rack of clothes around it. We continue to shiver. But from the moment the pains start Beatrice forgets the spartan conditions. Her moans take on an intensity that scares me. What do I know of what's normal in the world of childbirth? What if something goes wrong and it's all my fault?

When I eventually get through to the nursing home they tell me to bring her in straight away. The crescendos of screams on the journey have convinced me my sister's death is imminent, so it's a relief to hand her over to two uniformed staff who dismiss her histrionics with, 'That's quite enough of *that*, Mrs Mannering.'

It takes George eleven hours to negotiate his way in the blackout from Edinburgh through the unmarked roads and diversions to the nursing home. Until then I sit alone in the reception area.

A woman in a high starched cap greets him curtly in spite of the soft Irish accent, 'And would you be after being the father?'

George simply nods, keeping his eyes on the floor, for all the world like a man embarrassed by his part in this whole business.

'Sure. Right. Will you ever wait out here then, with your sister-in-law. We'll come and tell you when it's over.'

When there's no one about we clutch hands, urging each other to hold our nerve. Footsteps force us apart and we sit primly, waiting for news.

'At least you'll soon be home now,' he mutters. It's been hard for me too being parted from him so long and so soon into our marriage. Beatrice has been petulant. The landlady has been suspicious. My conscience has been troubled by the lack of useful wartime occupation. But George knows little of that; I want him to want this baby.

An hour drags by. Two. Three. Still no news. Four. Four and a half. Every one an eternity.

The regimental click of heels makes us both sit upright. We draw the veil back over our frightened eyes.

There's no smile, no kindness in her manner. 'It's all over. You can come in now, but I should warn you, your wife's exhausted. Don't be surprised if she's asleep by the time you get in there.'

She turns on her heel and marches back down the corridor. George and I tiptoe along behind her, keeping a respectable distance from each other.

'Right now, Doris,' she says bracingly. 'Here's your husband come to see you and the child. Are you after showing him what you've got?'

Beatrice looks unrecognisable. Her face is bloated and bruised. Her hair clings to her head as if she's been out in a thunderstorm. The bed is neatly made around her, the frills of my new nightdress peak above the sheet, but all I see are her eyes. Staring, vacant. She gives no sign of recognition or of welcome.

'Come on now, Doris, your sister's been after waiting outside ever since you came in and your husband's been here hours too. Sure, the least you can do is let them have a little look, don't you think?'

Still nothing from my sister.

The midwife waits a moment more, then bends to pick up the baby from the cot beside the bed.

'Well, here you are, Mr Mannering. You have a little girl. Mummy says her name's to be Jessica. Jessica Marina.'

George peers into the bundle of blankets with a stunned expression which makes me want to giggle.

Instead I creep closer until I can just see what's visible of this new member of our family. Wide dark eyes, a frown creasing the forehead, the tip of a tongue lapping against the lips. Splayed fingers close over the edge of the blanket. Perfect miniature fingernails.

'Oh George, look at her,' I whisper.

Before he can reply the midwife whisks the baby out of reach, talking as she goes. 'Now, Doris says she doesn't want to feed the child herself. We don't approve of bottles in here, but she insists. Sure, it's because she's so tired. So I must ask you to go now and give your wife some peace. We'll give baby Jessica a bottle this time, but we need Mummy to regain her strength so she can give the child what nature intended.'

I'm flabbergasted by the inference that it's entirely George's fault that Beatrice is exhausted. I want to leap to his defence, shout out his heroism. But of course, I can't.

If the midwife thinks it odd that the brand new parents neither speak nor touch, she gives nothing away. But wartime changes relationships. Partings, meetings... who knows what tomorrow will bring? And the staff neither know nor ask about this one.

Some things are simply best left unsaid.

Ten days later the borrowed car coughs its way from Inverness to Edinburgh. Negotiating the unfamiliar roads and controls requires all George's concentration. Beatrice is too preoccupied, I am too overawed, so for most of the journey we travel in silence. The baby, Jessica Marina, is now in my arms, for as soon as the doors of the nursing home closed behind us Beatrice and I exchanged roles.

We return to Edinburgh a new family. George and Doris Mannering and their new baby daughter born 10 months and 25 days after their wedding. A certificate to prove it. Aunt Beatrice in attendance. All very decent and in order.

Beatrice, now 17, will begin work next week in a munitions factory far from us, where no one knows her. Her choice. She wants to see as little as possible of Jessica.

My parents want to contribute to their granddaughter's maintenance; George refuses categorically. 'If she's to be my daughter, she's my responsibility.'

This man I married has depths and strengths I never dreamed of a year ago. How can I ever repay him?

Postscript

DAY ELEVEN.

'More wine, Mrs Wiseman?'

I'm toying with the honey roast duck with apricot stuffing, acutely aware of Aaron's foot stroking mine under the table. But when I sneak a glance he's not even looking at me. He's grinning at someone behind me.

'I'm afraid my wife seems rather preoccupied tonight. More wine, darling?'

'Oh I'm so sorry. Yes, please.'

As soon as the waiter moves away Aaron leans forward and whispers, 'You realise he's now convinced you're my mistress, don't you? He thinks the ring is a fake and the signature a forgery and he's probably contemplating sending an incriminating photograph to my home address.'

I grimace. He reaches across to lay a hand over mine.

'*You* may not respond to your new name but I have to tell you, I'm loving the sound of it. Revelling in the fact that my legally wedded wife is actually here alone with me, hundreds of miles away from all responsibilities, no one to distract her or give her an excuse to leave.'

'I don't want an excuse. Ever again.'

He lets his eyes answer for him.

I'm fighting to avoid comparisons. Of course, a month in

Canada in the best of hotels eclipses a week in Brighton in a seedy bed-and-breakfast. But we are 40 years on. The circumstances are entirely different. The world is a much more accessible place. And Aaron has four decades as a successful lawyer behind him; he isn't a young joiner augmenting his income teaching the basics of oboe-playing to reluctant children.

Eleven days so far, every one memorable. Seventeen more to come. We're in tune mentally, psychologically, emotionally.

Eleven nights so far... only now do I know what I've missed. Surely it isn't wrong to savour this contentment. I can only truly value my present happiness by measuring it against the past.

I don't deserve this second chance but it came anyway.

Aaron has a much more robust sense of what we deserve than I do. Lying beside me, he's admiring my wedding ring. He says it helps him register the 'legitimacy' of sharing my bed.

'Penny for them.'

'I was thinking about Mother, actually.'

'Nice thoughts?'

'All the treatments and preventions that have been promoted since she went into The Morningside: infrared helmets, crossword puzzles, nicotine... that new drug... what was it called? Ah yes, Rember.'

'And then there was MTC, taking statins, controlling fatty acids...'

'And that epilepsy drug, and vitamins...'

'And milk, and wine...'

'So that's why you've been plying me with the best Bordeaux.'

'Oh no,' he laughs,' I have a much more short-term reason than that!'

'And there was surfing the Internet – that was supposed to slow it down. And extra virgin olive oil.'

'We missed out embryonic stem cells. But as far as we know nothing has really come to anything, has it?'

'I know. And deep down, I don't believe it would have been

a kindness to prolong her life.'

'But being you, you have to question your motives and beat yourself up for not doing enough.' He sighs. 'Will you ever be truly happy?'

'Oh but I *am* happy, Aaron. I *am*... Ah, I fell for it again.'

He grins and gives me a hug. 'Sorry. Can't resist winding you up sometimes. But curiously enough, *I've* been thinking about your mum, too. I owe her a lot.'

'You do?' Held this close I can't see his expression.

'Mm. If she hadn't been so unselfish my mother wouldn't have remembered her. If Mother hadn't spoken of her in such glowing terms my curiosity wouldn't have been piqued. Without the big secret you wouldn't have had the same air of mystery.'

'So it's my family story not me you fell for.'

'Ahh, you've rumbled me! But of course, as you very well know, it was only *after* I met you that I mentioned your name to her. I was already smitten. But to return to what I was saying... if I hadn't known the standard your mum set, I might have misconstrued my first dismissal and never returned for a second chance.'

'But that presupposes that I inherited her unselfishness. And as we both know, I didn't inherit anything from her.'

'Oh yes you did,' he says softly.

'How come?'

He rears up on one elbow and looks into my eyes with an expression that makes my heart lurch.

'You have to be one of the most unselfish people I've ever met. And one of the most conscientious and responsible.'

'Mum was more so. And she definitely had a nicer nature than me.'

'If you say so. I can't judge. But that's the legacy she gave you. Not her genetic makeup. Her example. Which you chose to follow. Because you had a choice and, luckily for me, you turned yourself into the person you are. The woman I adore.'

'To think I nearly lost you for good.' I shudder in spite of the warmth around me. 'I really thought you'd be snapped up by some other more available woman.'

'I wasn't in the market for some other available woman. I'd already found what I was looking for.'

Much later he says, 'Now you've had time to get used to the idea, how do you feel about Beatrice being your real mother?'

'She isn't. She simply gave birth to me. Doris was my real mother. I see that now. And even if I'd known the truth a long time ago, I'd have done exactly what I did.'

'I believe you would.'

'Look what she did for me after all.'

He half-smiles.

'And I don't want Aunt Beatrice to spoil my memories. That's why I'm not going to tell her that I know about her.'

'I can understand that.'

'Imagine her claiming James as her grandson…'

'A wise decision all round. And you know, I rather like the idea of the two of us sharing this secret.'

A thought strikes me.

'When I found those photos in the cupboard under the stairs, I felt so sad. Rootless. I wasn't the me I thought I was. These people weren't my ancestors. But now we know I'm Beatrice's daughter, I'm back in that family tree.'

'Just in a different place.'

'Exactly.'

'But much more importantly, you are now in *my* family tree.'

I reach up to trace the outline of his face.

'I don't deserve you, Aaron Wiseman.'

'You deserve every happiness that comes your way, Jessica Wiseman. You've more than earned it.'

'Jessica Wiseman,' I repeat slowly. 'A lifetime ago I wrote that name on an envelope. It was one of those nights when Mother couldn't sleep and I was sitting beside her bed to stop her wandering. I sat for an age looking at the words. Like a love-sick teenager.'

'And then?'

'I burned it. It made me so unhappy.'
'And now?'
'It's still too good to be true. I can't believe it's me.'
'As the waiter downstairs knows!'

Remember Remember
Discussion Points for Bookclubs

- What is the purpose of the prologue in this book?

- If you only heard Jessica's side of the story what misconceptions would you retain?

- Doris' story unravels backwards in time. Why do you think the author chose this technique? How effective is it?

- Doris used to be first on Pandora's 'prayer list'. She has now 'consigned her grandmother to the past tense'. Why? What are the implications of this?

- Jessica is more disturbed by her father's part in the big deception than her mother's. Why is this? What do you think of his response to the question she asked as a child in the garden?

- Recalling her mother's suppressed grief, Jessica asks: 'All the anger I see in her now, all the fear, is it the emotion finding expression at last?' What do you think?

- In the second half of the book we get an explanation for many of Doris' behaviours. Does this change your feelings about her? Would knowing change the attitude of her carers?

- 'Step by step she has sunk down to the basement of her being,' Jessica says of her mother. Why do you think the author chose this analogy?

- Doris uses her own names for the carers. What other devices are employed to give the reader insight into Doris' perceptions when she is unable to communicate effectively? Which is the most effective for you?

- Doris and Jessica share certain experiences – losing a brother at a young age, having a selfish sister, being a driven person. Why do you feel the author added this extra potential for confusion?

- What new insights into dementia did you gain from this book?

If you are interested in further information about medical ethics or this series of books, visit the author's website and weekly blog. The website provides further discussion questions for students and teachers of medical ethics; an author profile; details of her books and the ethical topics covered in them; and links to related websites.

www.hazelmchaffie.com
www.VelvetEthics.com

Right to Die
Hazel McHaffie
ISBN 1 906307 21 0 PBK £12.99

Was it only two days ago? Seems like two hundred years. I was still in work mode then. Adam O'Neill, investigative journalist, columnist, would-be novelist. Researching my material. Amassing facts. And today? Yep. Sitting here consciously absorbing it, it's a totally different kettle of fish.

Naomi is haunted by a troubling secret. Struggling to come to terms with her husband's death, her biggest dread is finding out that Adam knew of her betrayal. He left behind an intimate diary – but dare she read it? Will it set her mind at rest – or will it destroy the fragile control she has over her grief?

Caught by the unfolding story, Naomi discovers more than she bargained for. Adam writes of his feelings for her, his challenging career, his burning ambition. How one by one his dreams evaporate when he is diagnosed with a degenerative condition, Motor Neurone Disease. How he resolves to mastermind his own exit at a time of his choice... but time is one luxury he can't afford. Soon he won't be able to do it alone. Can he ask a friend, or even a relative, to commit murder?

Adam's fierce determination to retain control of his own body against insurmountable odds fills his journal with a passion and drive that transcend his situation, and transfix the reader. A startlingly clear-sighted and courageous story, this novel explores the collision between uncompromising laws, complex loyalties and human compassion.

Lively and intensely readable... ALEXANDER MCCALL SMITH

The Bower Bird
Ann Kelley
ISBN 1 906307 98 9
(children's fiction)
PBK £6.99
ISBN 1 906307 45 8
(adult fiction)
PBK £6.99

Inchworm
Ann Kelley
ISBN 1 906817 12 X
PBK £6.99

I had open-heart surgery last year, when I was eleven, and the healing process hasn't finished yet. I now have an amazing scar that cuts me in half almost, as if I have survived a shark attack.

Gussie is twelve years old, loves animals and wants to be a photographer when she grows up. The only problem is that she's unlikely to ever grow up.

Gussie needs a heart and lung transplant, but the donor list is as long as her arm and she can't wait around that long. Gussie has things to do; finding her ancestors, coping with her parents' divorce, and keeping an eye out for the wildlife in her garden.

Winner of the 2007 Costa Children's Book Award.

It's a lovely book – lyrical, funny, full of wisdom. Gussie is such a dear – such a delight and a wonderful character, bright and sharp and strong, never to be pitied for an instant. HELEN DUNMORE

I ask for a mirror. My chest is covered in a wide tape, so I can't see the clips or incision but I want to see my face, to see if I've changed.

Gussie wants to go to school like every other teenage girl and find out what it's like to kiss a boy. But she's just had a heart and lung transplant and she's staying in London to recover from the operation.

Between managing her parents' love lives, waiting for her breasts to finally start growing, and trying to hide a destructive kitten in her dad's expensive bachelor pad, Gussie makes friends with another cardio patient in the hospital and finds out that she can't have everything her heart desires...

A great book. THE INDEPENDENT

This is definitely one of my top ten books. You have to read it, and it will stay with you forever! TEEN TITLES

The Burying Beetle
Ann Kelley
ISBN 1 84282 099 0
PBK £9.99
ISBN 1 905222 08 4
PBK £6.99

Bodywork
Dilys Rose
ISBN 1 905222 93 9
PBK £8.99

Meet Gussie. Twelve years old and settling into her new ramshackle home on a cliff top above St Ives, she has an irrepressible zest for life. She also has a life-threatening heart condition. But it's not in her nature to give up. Perhaps because she knows her time might be short, she values every passing moment, experiencing each day with humour and extraordinary courage.

Gussie's story of inspiration and hope is both heartwarming and heartrending. Once you've met her, you'll not forget her. And you'll never take life for granted again.

Gussie fairly fizzles with vitality, radiating fun and enjoyment into everything that comes her way. Her life may be predestined to be short but not short on wonder, glee, the love of things as they really are. It is rare to find such tragic circumstances written about without an ounce of self-pity. Rarer still to have the story of a circumscribed existence escaping its confines by sheer force of personality, zest for life.
MICHAEL BAYLEY

How do we feel about the flesh that surrounds us and how do we deal with the knowledge that it will eventually do so no more? How do our bodies affect our emotional, physical and spiritual lives?

Winner of the 2006 McCash prize, Dilys Rose's third collection of poetry focuses on the human body in all its glory, comedy and frailty; on the quirks, hazards and conundrums of physiology; on intimations of mortality – and immortality. Rose draws fully-grown characters in a few vivid strokes; from a body double to a cannibal queen, their souls are personified in a limb, affliction or skill. These poems get under your skin and into your bones – you'll never look at the human body in the same way again!

Dilys Rose exposes and illuminates humanity with scalpel sharpness... ingeniously exciting, quirky and perceptive. JANET PAISLEY, THE SCOTSMAN

It's an extraordinary book, brave and unusual, full of unexpected insights and delights – and a consistent compassion, respect and reverence for the human body, in all its oddity and complexity. CATHERINE SMITH

The Fatal Sleep

Peter Kennedy
ISBN 1 905222 67 X
HBK £20.00

Napiers History of Herbal Healing

Tom Atkinson
ISBN 1 905222 01 7
PBK £8.99

The bite of the tsetse fly – a burning sting into the skin – causes a descent into violent fever and aching pains. Severe bouts of insomnia are followed by mental deterioration, disruption of the nervous system, coma and ultimately death.

Sleeping sickness, also known as human African trypanosomiasism, is one of Africa's major killers. It puts 60 million people at risk of infection, occurs in 36 countries in sub-Saharan Africa, and claims the lives of many thousands of people every year.

Transmitted by the tsetse fly, trypanosomiasis affects both humans and cattle. The animal form of the disease severely limits livestock production and farming, and in people the toxic effects of the treatment can be as painful and dangerous as the disease itself. Existing in the shadow of malaria and AIDS, it is an overlooked disease, largely ignored by pharmaceutical companies and neglected by the western world.

This is a remarkable book. It is filled in equal measure with passion for science and compassion for the people afflicted with this cruel disease. SIR ROGER BANNISTER

What are black spleenwort, figwort and toadflax and how are they traditionally used?

How did Scottish herbalism develop from its crude Celtic roots into widely-used alternative medicine?

In what ways has the practice of herbalism changed in modern times from the Victorian world in which Duncan Napier founded Napiers?

Herbalism is the oldest form of medicine in the world. It has been practised for thousands of years, and is still the most widely-used method of healing in existence. This concise history reveals the development of herbalism through the ages, a unique journey from Neolithic Kurdistan to present-day Edinburgh.

It also contains the casebook and autobiography of Duncan Napier, a Victorian practitioner of herbal medicine, with notes from a modern herbalist. From the creation of Lobelia Syrup for coughing to the 48 foot tapeworm, the history of Napiers makes for fascinating reading.

Luath Press Limited

committed to publishing well written books worth reading

LUATH PRESS takes its name from Robert Burns, whose little collie Luath (*Gael.*, swift or nimble) tripped up Jean Armour at a wedding and gave him the chance to speak to the woman who was to be his wife and the abiding love of his life. Burns called one of the 'Twa Dogs' Luath after Cuchullin's hunting dog in Ossian's *Fingal*. Luath Press was established in 1981 in the heart of Burns country, and is now based a few steps up the road from Burns' first lodgings on Edinburgh's Royal Mile. Luath offers you distinctive writing with a hint of unexpected pleasures. Most bookshops in the UK, the US, Canada, Australia, New Zealand and parts of Europe, either carry our books in stock or can order them for you. To order direct from us, please send a £sterling chequ postal order, international money order or your credit card details (number, address of cardholder and expiry date) to us at the add below. Please add post and packing as follows: UK – £1.00 per delivery address; overseas surface mail – £2.50 per delivery address; overseas airmail – £3.50 for the first book to each delivery address, plus £1.00 for each additional book by airmail to the same address. If your order is a gift, we will happily enclose your card or message at no extra charge.

Luath Press Limited
543/2 Castlehill
The Royal Mile
Edinburgh EH1 2ND
Scotland
Telephone: 0131 225 4326 (24 hours)
Fax: 0131 225 4324
email: sales@luath. co.uk
Website: www. luath.co.uk